# MARIA, JUST MARIA

## Praise for the Book

'Will there be anything left if madness is taken away from life and from art? Madness is creativity as well as an effort to escape from the shackles of society, even as the mad person remains "just" another human being. A self-inquiry steeped in materiality makes Sandhya Mary's debut *Maria, Just Maria* a rare novel and Maria a literary character with a difference. Jayasree Kalathil's brilliant translation adds to its richness.'

– S. HAREESH, author of *Moustache*, winner of the 2020 JCB Prize for Literature

'Jayasree Kalathil brings her expert ear to this flawless and confident translation of the complex voice of a mad woman. A must-read!'

– DAISY ROCKWELL, translator of *Tomb of Sand* by Geetanjali Shree, winner of the 2022 International Booker Prize

# MARIA, JUST MARIA

## SANDHYA MARY

Translated from
the Malayalam by Jayasree Kalathil

*An Imprint of HarperCollins Publishers*

First published in English in India by Harper Perennial 2024
An imprint of HarperCollins *Publishers*
4th Floor, Tower A, Building No. 10, DLF Cyber City,
DLF Phase II, Gurugram, Haryana – 122002
www.harpercollins.co.in

2 4 6 8 10 9 7 5 3 1

Originally published in Malayalam as *Maria Verum Maria*
by Mathrubhumi Books, Kozhikode © Sandhya Mary 2018
This English translation © Jayasree Kalathil 2024

P-ISBN: 978-93-5699-377-8
E-ISBN: 978-93-5699-390-7

This is a work of fiction and all characters and incidents described in this book are the product of the author's imagination. Any resemblance to actual persons, living or dead, is entirely coincidental.

Sandhya Mary asserts the moral right
to be identified as the author of this work.

All rights reserved. No part of this publication may be reproduced, stored in a retrieval system, or transmitted, in any form or by any means, electronic, mechanical, photocopying, recording or otherwise, without the prior permission of the publishers.

Typeset in 11.5/16 Adobe Caslon Pro at
Manipal Technologies Limited, Manipal

Printed and bound at
Replika Press Pvt. Ltd.

This book is produced from independently certified FSC® paper to ensure responsible forest management.

# Contents

**PART I**

1. Some Thoughts About Life, and About Madness    3
2. I Became Mad Because…    15

**PART II**

3. Maria's Land    29
4. Kottarathil Veedu, Its Inhabitants and Little Maria    31
5. The Sorrows of Geevarghese Sahada    59
6. Kariyakutty Who Should Have Been a Saint, and Neena Who Became One    67
7. Geevarghese's Story    81
8. Chirammel Kathanar and the Family History of Kottarathil Veedu    103
9. Maria's Social Life    108

10. A Day in the Life of Little Maria in
    Kottarathil Veedu                                      115
11. Kuncheriya's Doubts and Dilemmas About Heaven          125
12. Anne, Mathew, Lisa … and Maria                         129
13. Maria Decides to Grow Up                               137
14. Maria Is Given Back                                    140
15. Maria's Return                                         160

### PART III

16. Thus, Too, Some Lives                                  165
17. Kottarathil Veedu, Appachan and Ammachi                187
18. Maria's Scattered Thoughts, Dreams, Life               192
19. The Dream that Is Kuttappayi                           205
20. Hari's Departure, and Vinayakan's                      210
21. About the Book Maria Wrote, or Is Going to Write       214

*P.S. Section*                                             219

*Acknowledgements*                                         233

# Part I

# 1

# Some Thoughts About Life, and About Madness

*When I woke up, I was still travelling. All through that night I travelled, taking my injured husband – ex-husband – with me. It all seemed to me like part of a surrealist movie shot in sepia tones. 'What was there between him and me…' That was my first thought when an unknown person called me to say that my husband had been injured. I found him lying on the verge of a dirt track cutting through the middle of a vast, arid plane. His right leg, severed at the knee, lay a few feet away. Blood and fluid still oozed from the wound, and the jagged edge of the bone protruded like a broken twig. It was only a leg, but it could have been cut with a bit more care, I thought. A flock of macaws, with wild expressions entirely unsuitable for their colourful bodies, tore at the exposed flesh. The pooled blood had dried in the merciless rays of the sun. He was crying loudly, but the moment he saw me, he said in a calm voice, 'If you could just fetch me my leg, I could go to work.' Without responding, I began walking towards his boss's shed a little distance away. I had two objectives: one, arrange a vehicle to take him to a hospital, and two, try and get some money from his employer. Not only did that unnaturally handsome and complete bore of a man deny me even a single paisa but the vehicle that arrived was a pick-up van instead of the ambulance I was expecting.*

*I had to take him to his village. But my mind told me that his family would not accept the responsibility of looking after him, and that this one-legged man would end up being my burden for the rest of his time. As I sat on the bare floor of the pick-up van and travelled through that desert-like place in the intense heat, I wished I loved him. It would have made this journey more meaningful.*

You must have come across such people, those who age prematurely for no apparent reason, who wake up from a night's sleep with faces lined with a lifetime of misery. Scientists say that our dreams last only for a few seconds, but for some people, there is unspeakable trauma in their dreams, the kind of trauma they would have never experienced in their waking lives, that drives them to madness.

When I woke up, I was in a deep pond of sorrow. Why did such unbearable dreams come in search of me?

When my brain finally adjusted to reality, I was Maria. Maria who had misplaced a few years of her life. Or, as Mama would say, Maria who had wasted her life; Maria who had wasted her time … Maybe I am wasting my time, but what else can I do with it? I have nothing else to do except to let it pass, let it go to waste. Who was it, I wonder, that discovered time was a thing to be used…

Earlier, my idea about life – not that I have given it much thought – was that being alive was something super. But now, when I think about life, what comes to mind is that clichéd bit of dialogue from Hollywood films: 'LIFE SUCKS'.

Human life up until the age of twenty is nothing to be taken seriously. All it amounts to is the sum total of ignorance, immaturity, stupidity, and above all else, arrogance. It doesn't matter if it is Isaac Newton, Shakespeare or Socrates, there is no one who does not think about some idiotic thing they did before they were twenty and say 'aiyye' with an embarrassed laugh. Those years, in short, are wasted. The twenties are the time for planning life and dreaming about it. In our thirties, we try to build something out of life as it unfolds. The best thing about the forties is that we come to certain realizations, and with a deep sigh we accept the most significant of them – that life is rarely as we dream of it. And along with it, we finally learn a lesson that makes living somewhat easier, that there is only this much to life. In short, the best thing about the forties is that we can apply the wisdom gained from the life lived thus far to the rest of our life, and we can spend our fifties with the help of this wisdom. The sixties bring with them various bodily ailments and their accompanying mental ailments, and by the seventies, old age sets in, heralding a time of loneliness, pain, helplessness and vulnerability, a time when even those who lived a grand life understand that their life has, in the final reckoning, amounted to nothing much. A time when we realize that we, as human beings, have lived life like a worm and will die like a worm. Even the most famous writers, scientists or politicians will find that their accomplishments are of no help. I would very much like to write a book about the old age of a political leader or a family man who has lived a completely autocratic life.

Footsteps…

Nurse Sushama arrives with a tray in her hand and a smile on her face.

'How are you today?'

I smile. Sushama places three tablets in my palm – yellow, blue and pink.

I look at those pills and think of Little Maria's A for Apple B for Ball C for Cat knickers. Yellow, blue and pink.

Then I think of Aravind. Aravind who painted mad pictures in deep colours. Aravind who has not been in my mad mind for the last few years.

It was by being able to see the remnants of my dreams that Aravind became an indelible mark in my life. This is how it began:

The guest in my dream that night was a camel. With a hump filled with life-giving water and an expression of disdain against the whole world, it insinuated itself into my dream. As soon as it entered, it smiled broadly at me and introduced itself as the one from the story of the Arab who had allowed his camel to share his tent. I noticed that it continued chewing even as it told me the story.

'The water in my hump is stored in a solid state,' it said as though it had read my mind. 'That's what I am chewing.'

'It's not ice,' it continued after a brief pause, but neglected to tell me what it was. 'Do you think there is anyone in this world who would willingly allow a camel inside his tent? No such thing has ever happened.'

With that, it sauntered out of my dream.

The next morning, Aravind told me: 'You know that story about the Arab and the camel? That's not how it happened. The tent was actually where the camel was tethered. The Arab, tired after having walked a long way, asked the camel for a little space inside to lie down. The camel obliged. But soon the Arab felt that it was too cramped to lie down properly. So, he told the camel that he would show him a small pond that never dried out, took it there and tied it to a tree, and went back and spent a comfortable night in the tent. The next day the Arab told everyone the story of the heartless camel who had usurped his tent.'

I imagine that the dog that walked out of my dream the other night would have gone straight into Aravind's dream. It was Yudhishthiran's dog, the companion of the eldest Pandava prince in the Mahabharatham. In my dream, the dog told me that the other four Pandava brothers had failed to sever their earthly ties and engage fully in the pursuit of heaven, and so were denied entry.

'Sahadevan worried about Kunthi, Nakulan about the fatherly love he was denied, Arjunan about Hastinapuri, and Bheeman about Panchali,' the dog told me. 'Yudhishthiran and I attained heaven because, in his intense desire to get there, he had forgotten all thought of earth, and I too had left nothing behind. But...'

The dog fell silent and sat there looking at me for a while. Then he walked out of my dream.

Although I desperately wanted to know the rest of what happened to Yudhishthiran's dog, I didn't tell anyone about it. Because everyone says that my mind is abnormal. That is how I ended up in this hospital. Madness, like death, is not a big deal to the world at large. Death is 'the ultimate loss' to the person dying, but it is inconsequential to the rest of the world. This is true of madness too. There are so many stories and films about people confined in psychiatric hospitals. Madness is often an easy solution for writers to conclude a story, especially stories with a hero or heroine in the grip of an existential crisis. And in comedy films, with some added exaggeration, it provides material to make the audience laugh. This, in short, is the world's relationship with madness. In real life, though, madness is boring. No, actually real life is boring and madness might add a bit of interest to it. But it is a pointless comparison because, ultimately, both are terribly boring. As for me, things were boring right from the start.

*I was 'it' then, before I became 'he' or 'she', the time when I floated around light as cotton.*

*I was a child who never wanted to be born. And when I was born, the shock of unexpectedly finding myself confined within a human form remained in me. Maybe that was why, as an infant, I did not inspire people to exclaim, 'Yyoda chakkara! What a sweet little thing!'*

*To be honest, as I slid down a tunnel from the prison that was the womb, I was expecting to float away again. But it was an even bigger prison that awaited me at the end of that tunnel.*

*I am amazed when I hear people wax nostalgic about 'mother's womb'. I think it is a masculine thing – this nostalgia. I don't think women spend time thinking about their mothers' wombs. Poor things, men! Tender as touch-me-nots!*

*Having entered the prison outside, I was uneasy. People came up to me with the normal facial expressions reserved for newborns, but their smiles and affection quickly transformed into concern when they saw the expression on my face – anger, irritability. Their touch caused me actual pain.*

*I was dozing off in a short interval of no pain. I was dreaming that I was floating around as before, and a super-beautiful angel flew up to me and gave me a super-beautiful smile. When I came out of that dream and opened my eyes, I saw the angel right in front of my face, smiling at me. I smiled back.*

*'Edee, look, the child is smiling at me! Come, look!' the angel said, startling me with his excitement. Then I heard another voice.*

*'You've lost your mind! Children don't smile as soon as they are born!'*

*By then, having been startled by the angel, my face had settled into its usual expression. So, when the owner of the second voice came to check, what they saw was me lying there with my scowling face.*

*That angel was Appachan.*

Anyway, I am getting back to normal now. They say that is why I have begun to remember things. That must be true, because the other day I woke up remembering an interesting episode from my marriage.

I shocked my parents, first by getting married to a man I loved. Then, when they had begun to accept the fact, I shocked them again by getting divorced.

'What's the problem?'

'This is not what I want.'

'Didn't you know that before?'

'I realized this was not what I wanted only when I understood what this was.'

My husband was also shocked when I told him I wanted out of the marriage. What I really meant was that I wanted out of all marriage, married life in general.

Then followed the expected questions and the not-so-expected answers...

'But why?'

'I want to be happy.'

'Aren't you happy now?'

'Sometimes yes, and at other times, no.'

'You do realize that's just how life is, don't you?'

'That's how life is as we know it. Another life should be possible.'

'So, are you saying you can't be happy with me?'

'Not just with you, with anyone.'

'You're being selfish by considering only your happiness.'

'Not at all. I am doing this because I want to show others, everyone, that another kind of happiness is possible.'

'Are you mad?'

It is funny when you think about it. Me, with my crazy head, was going to show the world that another life was possible ... Honestly! I feel I should apologize to my ex-husband.

'Shall I switch on the TV?' Sushama asks.

I nod. It has only been a few days since I got the TV in my room. As far as the inmates of this hospital are concerned, TV marks a milestone in their lives. Normally, we are not allowed to watch TV because the programmes would upset our tender minds. That they have allowed a TV in my room is proof that they believe I am on the mend, that I am normal adjacent.

The scenes on TV look exactly like those from the serials Saralachechi used to watch. The same women ... the same silk saris ... the same crying.

'But Sushama, this one seems just like that old serial...'

'It's actually the same one!'

'You mean they have gone on crying all these years?'

Sushama hands me the remote control and leaves. After so many years, the TV is my first companion, even though it had played an equal part, along with Appachan, Mathiri valyammachi and Chandippatti, in causing damage to my brain.

The serial makes me sad. I begin to miss Saralachechi, Radhika and Nimmi, and the big house where I had found peace. And more than anyone else, I miss Aisha. Aisha who had hated men, and then decided to live with a man anyway.

I cannot bear the sadness in the serial any more, so I switch to a news channel. The first piece of news I hear after many years is this: 'American president receives a grand welcome in India.' My mind anticipates the image of a smiling George Bush coming down the steps of the aeroplane into the melee of cameras.

The aeroplane and the cameras are exactly as I imagine, but the person who comes down the airstair with a broad smile on his face is a black man. 'These idiotic channels!' That is my first thought. But I quickly realize that in the few years I had lost hold of my mind, America had elected its first African American president.

This man, Barack Obama, who I am seeing for the first time, disturbs me. I think of Karthav Eesho Mishiha, Our Lord Jesus Christ, and the revolution of black people and all marginalized people that we had planned together. I watch this man – black-skinned but with the expressions and mannerisms of a proper white-skinned person – and think: 'He has made my revolution redundant.'

Soon, though, my post-madness mind realizes, with a deep sense of nostalgia, that Karthav and the revolution we had planned together were products of my madness. I look at Him on the wall and tell myself, with the same sense of nostalgia, that it is only a picture. I am equally angry at Obama and at Karthav, and I feel like crying.

I was aware by then that normal people don't cry over such foolishness. So, with great difficulty, I control my tears. I am sure that if I stopped myself from crying for a whole hour, I would win this battle. But is it necessary to win battles with such difficulty? Is this what everyone calls normal, practical life?

I am desperate to talk to someone. Aravind is too far away. And Appachan ... Appachan was in the earth, hunched and frozen in his grave. I remember the Maria who sat on the wet mud and hit it with her fist after Appachan was put under it.

To escape the sea of sorrow, I walk out of my room. On the veranda, Captain Vijayaraghavan and Sunanda teacher stand together as usual.

Sunanda teacher lost her mind after the death of her three children...

Water was the villain in her story. Her oldest son, who had won several trophies for swimming, had drowned in a river. Her second child – a nine-year-old daughter – died in a boating accident. News channels had milked the incident for all it was worth as several small children had lost their lives. From then on, Sunanda teacher began to fear rivers. It was hard to have a third child, but she did, eventually – a smart little boy. She refused to let him see rivers even from afar, banished them from their lives, and brought him up in a house secured within high boundary walls. But his destiny was to drown in the water tank in the yard when he was only two years old.

Captain Vijayaraghavan was a man who had to pay the price for patriotism with his sanity. All he had ever wanted to do was to be a soldier, one who protected his country and his people. Many were the childhood dreams in which he had vanquished imaginary enemies and saved his motherland, and when he grew up, he joined the army to realize those dreams. In the thirty-odd years that followed, he witnessed several large and small encounters and countless deaths including those of his close friends. Now, even the smallest sound terrifies him and makes him run for cover.

What I am trying to say is that everyone here has a reason for their madness – everyone except me. I became mad without a clear and concise reason. My madness is the result of a careless mind, and because of it, I see myself as beneath everyone else here.

Despite being surrounded by mad people, this hospital is a good place to live. It is only the sense of calmness that pervades the place that would make you wonder whether this was a psychiatric hospital. I can live here comfortably as long as my brother Mathew continues to pay the bills. He is a successful doctor in America. Still, one can't say how long his wife will let him squander away his money.

I don't usually step out of my room. What is the point in hanging out with these mad people? But when it is dark, it is difficult. The sounds of the night, especially the song of the cicada, irritate me. Aravind and I have a friend, Vinayakan, who is the one who pointed out that the cicada makes one of the loudest noises – occha – of all creatures. It should have been called occhu, but that name is given to the slow, soundless snail. Malayalam is a crazy language, he used to say. That, in fact, is one of the most intelligent comments I have ever heard. Vinayakan is a great chess player, but he went totally mad and now just wanders around. Chess is dangerous that way. It makes us use our brains way too intensely until the brain gets fed up and pisses off. I guess now you'll ask me how come Viswanathan Anand is not mad. Well, have you looked at his face? There is no way he will ever be mad. Anand is very practical and controlled, like a computer system. He even knows that *this* part of the brain should be used seventy per cent while *that* part should be used thirty per cent. I am not saying this because I have watched Anand play chess. In fact, I don't know chess. I know this because it is written on his face. But Bobby Fischer was troubled like Vinayakan. Take note when people respond to questions with 'I don't know', that is an important sign of madness, the inability to be decisive.

About Vinayakan's madness ... In addition to abusing his brain, he also partakes of all the drugs in the world. He used to go to the Himalayas once every six months in search of top quality charas. Sometimes he would stay there for a long time. He doesn't have relatives like my brother Mathew, so he is still free to wander the wide world with his mad head. He tried teaching me chess once, but I knew I couldn't get it because I am incapable of concentrating on anything for more than a minute.

Nothing I have said about Vinayakan and his madness is exactly true. The fact is that his normal state of being is what others call madness, and when he realized this fact, he embraced it. This is true of ninety per cent of mad people. It is when they adapt to a state of being that is most suited to who they are that we start calling them mad. I don't know about people who become violent when mad – I don't usually understand anything to do with violence.

As for *my* madness...

Several opinions exist on the subject of my madness.

Mama, my birth mother, says that she can't remember even a minute when I was not mad. 'She was born mad,' she told my doctor, 'I didn't waste much time thinking about it.'

Ammachi – she is actually Mama's ammachi and my grandmother – says Appachan is responsible for my madness.

Then there is Mathew, trying continuously to convince me and himself that I am not mad. From the time we were children, he stood careful watch over my mad mind and mad life even though he knew it was pointless. The funny thing is that he often slips my mind!

And Aravind ... he says I became mad when I was born. Poor Aravind! I wanted to marry him.

# 2

# I Became Mad Because...

In my opinion, I became mad because of Appachan's departure. Appachan – Mama's appachan, actually, and my grandfather – did not die; he went away.

This is how it began.

I had to prepare myself for two eventualities:

1. Appachan's departure.
2. My isolation.

Up until then, whether we were physically together or not, Appachan's spirit was always with me. Not performing miraculous deeds or anything, just making sure that I knew I was not alone. Like everyone else, I too had a family – Papa, Mama, siblings – but Appachan was the anchor of my life. So, to be perfectly honest, it was not his death but my imminent orphanhood that scared me the most. I felt guilty about my selfishness but, as I am sure you know, these are not feelings that are within our control. Appachan saw the terror on my face. 'Don't worry,' he said, 'I will always be with you, even after my death.'

The issue was this: I did not take the existence of the spirits of the dead all that seriously. For me, Appachan's spirit was something embedded in his material body. I did believe in spirits of the departed, but I saw them more as comical beings riding around on spears. Not that I thought the spear made them necessarily cruel or animalistic – I just took it to be an instrument they used for navigation. Also, I could not imagine that the spirits of Mathiri valyammachi, Kuncheriya valyappachan and Anna valyamma would possess positive qualities like love or empathy. As far as I was concerned, they had always been comical beings. So how could Appachan be any different?

'Listen, Maria,' Appachan said, holding my hand, 'I'm giving you an important responsibility. You must take me safely across to the Other World. You'll see many of our people along the way but avoid them all. You should hand me over only to Mathiri valyammachi. Do you understand?'

'Yes, Appacha.'

'Right, then. Hold on tight. Let's begin our journey.'

I liked the dramatic way in which he behaved at the time of his death.

On the first day, I did not see anyone special. Perhaps I was still outside the gravitational field of the Other World. Or perhaps I was not yet fully prepared mentally to enter that world.

I was not able to eat anything properly because I was holding on to Appachan's hand the entire time. The only consolation was the snacks Ammachi brought me from time to time. Ammachi was very practical and continued to take care of the affairs of the household, perhaps more efficiently than usual. The house was packed with relatives – Appachan and Ammachi's children, their children's children and so on – who had come to attend

Appachan's imminent death. Ammachi knew death was only an ordinary, if rare, event that occurred in every family. All that the rest of us could do was to ensure that the person about to die could do so in peace.

I was munching on a neyyappam held in my free hand when Appachan opened his eyes and looked at me. 'Maria,' he said in a serious voice, 'try and do the job you're given with a bit more integrity.'

I looked back and forth at Appachan and at the half-eaten neyyappam in my hand, not knowing what to do with it.

'Well, finish it then. Otherwise, you won't stop thinking about it.'

Those were Appachan's last words.

*I want to hug Mathiri valyammachi. But, unlike the mischievous person in my imagination, the person I see is a stern-faced old woman. She is not attractive to look at – I didn't really know whether she had been an attractive person because I have never seen a picture of her. She looks human but she reminds me of the alien creature in the movie,* ET, *except that the* ET *alien had a soft face whereas hers looks parched and has an expression like a smoke-cloud.*

*I begin to tell her about Appachan.*

*'I know,' she says, interrupting me.*

*'I'm your great-granddaughter, Geevarghese appachan's granddaughter.'*

*'Leave the thing here and go.'*

*'What thing?'*

*'The thing you brought.'*

*'Aiyo! That's not a thing, that's Appachan!'*

*'Yes, leave it here and go away.'*

'But Appachan is not a thing, Appachan is Appachan!'
'When you're in someone else's place, learn to respect what they say. I told you to leave it there, so just do so. Understood?'

'Yes. Here it is.'

I want to say 'Yes, Valyammachi', but refrain because I am afraid I might break some other rule.

The place is like a desert, windswept. Everything I see is two-dimensional, and the sights, well, images more like, appear and disappear at great speed only to be replaced by new ones.

'Why is everything here two-dimensional?' I ask Mathiri valyammachi, unable to contain my curiosity.

'Everything you see here is real. Reality is not attractive. But three-dimensional things never have the clarity of the two-dimensional.'

That much is true. Everything has a rare clarity, but the excessive clarity also makes them seem artificial.

'Mathiri valyammachi, were you like this before?' My curiosity gets the better of me again.

'I told you, the only thing that is real is what you see here,' she says, looking at me with her smoky eyes. 'What was before doesn't matter.'

And, like smoke, she disappears. I feel sad thinking about Appachan. My poor Appachan who had believed that the Other World would be something super. I feel an even greater sadness for myself. This has been the greatest disappointment of my life.

All I can do is cry about the loss of a beautiful dream. By then, within me, Appachan has transformed into something like a sackcloth bundle, a 'thing' like Mathiri valyammachi said. I sit in that place that was like an overly exposed black-and-white movie and begin to cry. Suddenly, a strong smell reminiscent of death – sandalwood joss sticks and frankincense – assaults my nose. Usually, the smell makes me faint, and even in the middle of crying, I feel anxious and apologetic about fainting in that unfamiliar place.

O Lord, God of my salvation,
when, at night, I cry out in your presence,
let my prayer come before you;
incline your ear to my cry.

For my soul is full of troubles,
and my life draws near to Sheol.
I am counted among those who go down to the Pit;
I am like those who have no help,
like those forsaken among the dead,
like the slain that lie in the grave,
like those whom you remember no more,
for they are cut off from your hand.
You have put me in the depths of the Pit,
in regions dark and deep.
Your wrath lies heavy upon me,
and you overwhelm me with all your waves.

You have caused my companions to shun me;
you have made me a thing of horror to them.
I am shut in so that I cannot escape;
my eye grows dim through sorrow.
Every day I call on you, O Lord;
I spread out my hands to you.
Do you work wonders for the dead?
Do the shades rise up to praise you?
Is your steadfast love declared in the grave,
or your faithfulness in Abaddon?

The first thing I heard was the sing-song voice of Sini – Mathachan valyappan's granddaughter – reading the Bible. The atmosphere, smoky from the burning joss sticks, frankincense and candles, made me gag. People rushed around in the smoke as the candles burned with a vengeance amidst the huge, ornate metal crucifixes brought over from the church.

And at the centre of it all, Appachan lay under a white sheet with an expression like a smoke-cloud on his face. There were no more battles to be fought on his behalf. His life was over; so was mine.

'This world is not real,' I shouted at Ammachi. 'And that real Other World? That's a cursed place.'

I ran out to the yard and vomited until my soul was purged, and when it was done, I felt famished. I went into the kitchen and began stuffing my mouth with whatever I could find. Ammachi says it was in that moment that she understood Maria had lost her mind. In truth, though, if she had remembered I had not eaten anything – except for that godforsaken neyyappam – for the last two days, she would have found my gluttony natural. When I returned from the kitchen, Appachan was still there with his smoke-cloud expression. 'Appacha…' I called out and ran to him and embraced him like I was mad. But no one thought it strange because a certain level of drama is allowed when death occurs.

I never touched Appachan after that because he had become 'it', 'the thing' so far away that I could not touch or know any more. I sat down on one of the chairs placed around his body, a little away from everyone else. Ammachi was flanked by two elderly valyammas, women who had made a habit, or a ritual, out of sitting in the front row with members of the close family even when they were not related to the deceased. I saw the shadowy shapes of my mama and Appachan's other children and grandchildren sitting or walking around. And suddenly, I caught sight of Anna valyamma, standing uncertainly behind Susanna aunty. As soon as she saw me, she came and sat down beside me.

'Who's that girl?' she asked, pointing at Sini.

'Sini,' I replied. 'Mathachan valyappan's granddaughter.'

Neither of us remembered the fact that Anna valyamma had been dead for many years.

'So, who are you?' Anna valyamma asked me the question she used to ask me all the time when she was in the grip of dementia.

'I'm Maria, Anna's daughter.'

She seemed satisfied with my response because she did not tell me, like she used to in the time of dementia, 'But I am Anna, and I don't have any daughters.'

'Poor Chettan,' she said, instead. 'He should go straight to heaven if you think about his life in this world, but who knows what happens after death!'

I realized that she thought the deceased was Appachan's appachan, Kuncheriya valyappachan, and not Appachan. She was still in the grip of dementia!

'Go and get me some kanjaalam from the kitchen,' Anna valyamma – who was known to everyone as 'Kanjaalam valyamma' when she was alive – told me. I told her that as this was a house where a death had occurred, they wouldn't be cooking rice, and so there wouldn't be any 'kanjaalam' – which is what she called kanjivellam, water in which the rice was boiled – to be had. That upset her, and she said with unnecessary sternness, 'Don't you know I can't live without kanjaalam?'

Ammachi came over and asked me who I was talking to. 'Anna valyamma,' I said, and Ammachi, ignoring that as the wife of the deceased she was supposed to sit right next to his body, took me to her room. Everyone seemed to be paying more attention to me than to Appachan who had just died. Ammachi tried her hardest to get me to sleep but I ignored her, and as soon as she left, I got out of the room and walked to the rubber plantation. I climbed to the top of the cashew nut tree where, as a young child, I used to sit looking out for Kuttappayi, my childhood heartthrob. People going by to pay their respects to Appachan looked over their shoulder at me in puzzlement.

All my life, I had never yearned for the touch of another person, but in that moment, I longed for someone to hold me close. I thought of Aravind.

## In Aravind's opinion, I became mad because…

*At the very first glance, I understood that Maria had lost what little grip on reality she had. She fell into my arms saying, 'Aravind, we need to rescue Appachan from that awful Other World.' I hugged her tightly, stroked her hair and kissed her. I was aware of the stares of the people around us, and yet I did everything I could to console her. My parents and my sister watched me and the mad woman who had come to me in the middle of the night. In the shock of the event, no one said anything.*

*Those were decisive moments as far as I was concerned, time when I had to convince myself and her, assuming she could still understand things, of the depth of my love for her. I told her everything I had refrained from saying when she could have understood me. I sat with her the whole night, holding her close, proving, in those moments, that I was worthy of her love.*

## Mathew's opinion

*The six-year-old picking up the piece of laddu I had thrown into the yard, dusting it up and putting it in her mouth, looking around, even* in her greed, to see if anyone was watching her. She was proud, almost arrogant, yet at that moment her face was suffused with the pain of the self-inflicted indignity even though no one else saw her shame. She was my little sister. I am aware that you might find these words unnecessarily dramatic and emotional, but I swear to you that is how it looked. A pulsating ache that will last till the end of my life – that is how Maria was etched in my heart.

With that sight, all the hatred I had accumulated towards Maria turned into a moist feeling. I don't know whether a handful of moments could change someone, especially a seven-year-old boy, so deeply, but that is what happened to me.

Maria was always an outsider in my home even though she was a member of our family just like the rest of us. Until she was around six, she grew up with Appachan in our grandparents' house while Anne, Lisa and I remained at home with Papa and Mama. Her life with Appachan was without structure or discipline, the life of a vagabond. I couldn't tell you for sure if her life turned out the way it did because she grew up with Appachan. Knowing Maria, she might have turned out this way even if she had lived with us instead.

After that incident, I began leaving snacks around the house for Maria. I would nibble at them a little and leave them where she would find them. Even today, she doesn't take anything herself to eat from our house because, as far as she is concerned, Appachan's house, not ours, is her house. I have never asked her about it.

Even after we grew up, the enmity between Lisa and Maria continued. She was not close to Anne either. I was away meanwhile, studying medicine. Still, I don't think Maria ran away because she felt isolated at home; she would have done it anyway. But at that time, I was not interested in her affairs. I was consumed with the thrill of studying medicine. My obsession with medicine had started the day, *when on a visit to Appachan's house, I had borrowed Shajan chachan's stethoscope and listened to the heartbeat of Maria's dog, Chandippatti. I had even planned to kill Chandippatti to teach Maria a lesson. I took him a plate of rice and meat curry laced with Furadan – everyone used to call it 'kurudaan' in those days. But he kicked it over and gave me a stern look that almost made me pee in my pants. From then on, every time he saw me, Chandippatti looked at me sideways as though warning me to behave. Everyone was sceptical about Maria's claim that Chandippatti was a special dog, but I think she might have been right. I am a doctor, I know, who should believe only in science. Still...*

*When I heard about Maria's marriage, I was entrapped in love myself, and other than feeling mildly surprised, I had no time for anything else. I did feel, also, slighted by the fact that Maria chose not to tell me about it. Knowing her, I should have forgiven her...*

## In my doctor's opinion, I became mad because...

The doctor gave his opinion to Aravind. On a rainless yet damp evening, Aravind came to the doctor, steeped in so much sorrow that he looked like a patient himself.

Aravind did not visit Maria. He could not bring himself to see Maria when she was in a state where she did not recognize him. After Maria was hospitalized, he went far away from the place, but no matter how far he went, his heart throbbed, ached. Hari was dead, Vinayakan had lost his mind, and Maria had lost hers. And Aravind with this love that he couldn't make sense of ... Aravind who had become isolated ... He felt that even the doctor of minds who sat in front of him could not understand him.

The doctor, despite having lived abroad for several years amassing degrees, spoke in a proper Thodupuzha dialect, making

Aravind wonder whether he was even a real doctor. 'Then again, he is a mad people's doctor,' he said to himself.

'They brought her here because she had given up speaking,' the doctor told Aravind. 'No matter how much we tried, she didn't speak for years. Then, one day, Chinnamma goes to give her food. "Listen," she says to Chinnamma, "I didn't speak because I didn't want to, not because I couldn't." And after a pause, she said, "Like Ammini."'

The doctor asked Aravind who Ammini was. Aravind thought of her, and how she had stopped speaking one day and started speaking again another day much later. And yet, he said, 'I have no idea.'

'Then she began to write,' the doctor continued. 'Like she was possessed by some kind of madness! Strange thing to say, right? How else would mad people write! Anyway, I went to see her on my rounds one day, and she held on to my hand and cried for almost an hour. Then suddenly she stopped, just like that, like it had been switched off. And with no sign of sadness, in a neutral voice, she spoke: "Yesterday an elephant died under my foot. It was mashed up, and pus oozed from it. The sad thing is that it was the elephant I had brought up with such good care…"

'I'll be honest. I almost believed her at first, you know. Like it had died trampled underfoot like a snail or a beetle. I even felt like getting her another elephant. After Maria became normal, I told her this elephant story. She listened to it, and in the same neutral voice, she said: "It wasn't like a snail or a beetle. The mashed-up elephant was more like a mussel that oozed pus."

'What I think is that Maria will always be like she is, must have always been like she is.'

For Aravind, Maria was a picture he wanted to draw but never could.

'Doctor, what you said about her writing ... where is it now?' he asked instead.

'Ah, yes. I went to her room one day and the dustbin was overflowing with papers. I asked her what they were, and she said they were all wastepaper. A psychiatrist's curiosity perhaps, I picked them up and brought them here.'

As he spoke, the doctor got up and opened an almirah, took out a large, untidy pile of paper, and handed it to Aravind.

# Part II

# 3
# Maria's Land

The fact is that the land where Maria was born was itself complicated. Complicated because it had no complex problems – no major natural disasters, or wars, or even epidemics. Having lived in such an atmosphere for generations, Maria's compatriots had a light-hearted attitude towards life. Politics and illicit sexual relationships were their favourite topics of discussion.

They thought of themselves as a people with keen political awareness. For example, those who involved themselves in the illegal business of dredging sand from riverbeds went to their jobs every day after reading all about its detrimental consequences in the morning's newspapers. And those in the granite quarrying business knew very well that levelling hills and blasting stones out of the earth destroyed not only the hills but the earth itself. The most important national festival of the land was the elections.

They discussed, astutely taking different sides of the argument, the military coup that happened in some faraway country they had not even heard of before. And as democracy progressed without major hitches in their own land, they craved the refreshing feel of autocracy.

They knew exactly who among their leaders were corrupt or implicated in sexual scandals, and yet these leaders held on to high positions in society with clear popular support. People debated these issues in toddy shops, chai shops and TV panel-shows.

For Maria's compatriots, politics was limited to those subjects in which politicians got involved. The TV channels in the land reported even the minor altercations – there were no major altercations to report – between the police and the students as 'Breaking News'. All occasions, including chance vehicle accidents, were celebrated onscreen.

They were great patriots. They stood at attention whenever they heard the national anthem. On Independence Day and on Republic Day, they decorated their vehicles with the national flag and watched the film *Gandhi* as though it was an age-old ritual.

Their children spoke English as though it was their mother tongue, and their parents listened, their skin covered in joyous goosebumps. They swallowed English medicines by the handful even when they had the common cold, and boasted that their quality of life was equal to that in America.

There was something else beyond all this that made them unique. In the elections that followed the Emergency, when the entire nation voted against the political party and its leader who had dragged the country through unspeakable horrors, this land was the only one that gave them a roaring victory.

In the map of the world, this land is known as Kerala.

It is where Maria was born.

# 4

# Kottarathil Veedu, Its Inhabitants and Little Maria

Little Maria and her dog, Chandippatti, were playing in the front yard of Kottarathil Veedu, the house that belonged to Geevarghese. It was with Geevarghese, Maria's appachan, her mother's father, that Maria lived during the first few years of her childhood. A heated argument progressed on the veranda between Sheena aunty and Thomachan chachan, her mother's siblings. Two more of her mother's siblings lived in Kottarathil Veedu – Neena aunty whom Maria disliked intensely, and Shajan chachan who was studying medicine in Thiruvananthapuram. The rest had spread out to different parts of the world after their marriage or because of work. The argument between Sheena and Thomachan was about the Emergency. Going against the traditional politics of Kottarathil Veedu, Sheena, who believed in communism, aimed bitter criticism against the Emergency, while Thomachan, a staunch Congress man, obviously defended it. His main point was that there was law and order in the country. Sheena countered it by saying that since pretty much everyone was imprisoned, law and order was only natural.

As she played, Little Maria had one ear tuned towards the argument. 'Thomachan chachan knows many things, but he is not as smart as Sheena aunty,' Maria thought. 'Besides, it's Sheena aunty who brings me snacks every day. So, what she says is right.'

'Who is that sitting on my chair?'

Little Maria did not have to turn around and look to know what might have happened. In the heat of the argument, Thomachan chachan had inadvertently sat down on Appachan's easy chair.

'Get out of my sight, both of you! Or I'll declare emergency right here.'

Geevarghese loved the word 'emergency' and used it willy-nilly even after the Emergency was over.

'Appacha, why do you scare them so?' Little Maria asked. 'They do make too much noise sometimes, but do you have to scold them?'

Two people watched all this: Geevarghese's father Kuncheriya who sat on the other easy chair in the veranda, and Anna on the swing Geevarghese had hung for Maria from a branch of the kotta mango tree. Maria's swing was now Anna's swing. But, despite her annoyance, Maria did not do anything about it because upsetting Anna would apparently worsen her dementia which was already in a serious state. Appachan said that we should treat those with dementia as though they were children. And because of it, eighty-year-old Anna usurped from five-year-old Maria all the attention, consideration, and more importantly, the snacks that should rightfully belong to the youngest in the family. Anna was a distant relative and had come to Kottarathil Veedu at a young age because of the poor financial circumstances of her own family.

In those days, Anna was famous as 'Kanjaalam valyamma' all around the neighbourhood. At every opportunity, she sneaked into the neighbouring houses begging for kanjaalam. She would drink it right then and there, and if she could not finish it, she would bring it back home in a bottle or a dish to have with her meals. Once, unable to stand the embarrassment, Mariyamma – Geevarghese's wife and Maria's grandmother whom she called Ammachi – locked her up in a room, but she had to let her out after Geevarghese made an almighty ruckus. Not satisfied, Geevarghese, in an inebriated state, made Mariyamma apologize to Anna.

Little Maria pretended not to hear Mariyamma calling her, repeatedly, to get ready for school. She hated the school where Devaki teacher waited for her with the cane. One wrong answer and Maria would be rewarded with the bitter medicine of the cane. Maria did not care about right or wrong answers, or why there were so many questions to be answered, and wondered where Devaki teacher found them. Besides, Devaki teacher did not let Chandippatti sit with Maria in the classroom, so he ran around in the school ground chasing after crows and cats until the school let out. Then, he snapped at a couple of girls and tore their skirts, and Devaki teacher banished him from the school compound. The first girl whose skirt Chandi took a bite of was Geetha, who had refused to share roasted tamarind seeds with Maria. The girl was so frightened, she ran away! That evening, Maria asked Chandippatti, 'Why did you tear her skirt?' Chandi somersaulted on the ground and said, 'That girl is so full of herself!' The second skirt Chandippatti tore into tatters belonged to Rani Padmini, the girl who always topped Maria's class, the daughter of Rathnamma teacher who taught Class 4. And with that, Chandi was banished from the school yard. That evening, too, Maria asked him, 'Why did you take a bite of Rani Padmini's skirt?' Chandi rolled over in the dirt and said, 'Oh, that girl is so full of herself!' The only thing that was good about the school compared to the house was that Anna valyamma wasn't there to annoy her.

Maria found school traumatic because she could not understand the psychology behind competitions, exams, being at the top of the class, or why some people were considered smart just because they knew the answers to specific questions asked at specific times. Did knowing the answers to questions make someone smart? But this was a question that only applied to others, as far as Maria was concerned. She had never considered herself to be smart, ever.

Maria had an aluminium box to take her books to school, and a small lunchbox made of steel. Its lid was tight, and Maria could never get it open. Sukesan opened it for her, banging it on the floor at a particular angle. And when opened, there would be rice topped with fried fish, chammanthi and achinga mezhukkupuratti that Ammachi had prepared. Sukesan would look at it, swallow his saliva, and go off to eat the upma, the free meal served up in the school kitchen. Maria, meanwhile, wanted to eat the upma but Mariyamma did not let her, saying that it was only for children from families that could not afford square meals. But Maria found a way around her objections. One day, when Sukesan opened her lunchbox for her and stood salivating over the mutta porichathu – eggs scrambled with onions and green chillies – inside, she told him: 'From now on, you eat my lunch and give me your upma.' The arrangement lasted until Maria was sent back to her parents' home.

While Maria and Sukesan found this arrangement highly satisfactory, there was someone who was most upset by it – Chandippatti. It was he who polished off her lunch after Maria dejectedly moved it around in the box for a bit. But ever since the school-upma-for-home-cooked-meal barter system was put in place, all he could do was watch, as his mouth watered, Sukesan gobble up the rice with the fried fish or the mutta porichathu. Chandippatti tried to tell Mariyamma about this development, but every time he opened his mouth, Mariyamma shouted, 'Scram, you dirty son of a bitch,' at him and pelted him with whatever she could lay her hands on. Mariyamma could not stand the sight of Chandippatti.

Something had happened a couple of years ago. One day, Kottarathil Veedu was burgled. The burglar was a dookly local thief who, in actual fact, was not really in the mood to attempt a burglary on that scorching afternoon. It was just that the quietness surrounding the house as everyone had their siesta and the front door that was left open were too much of a temptation. With the circumstances highly conducive, he went about his work in a relaxed manner.

Soon, as he rummaged through the house, he felt that someone was watching him. He tried to disregard the feeling at first, but when it became intense, he turned, and there was a dog watching his every move carefully! The thief, cowardly by nature, assumed that his luck was up and stood perfectly still as he realized he did not have even a penknife to defend himself with, cursing himself for being tempted to enter the house while on his way to the market to buy some tapioca. But the dog said nothing! He just stood there looking unblinkingly at the burglar. Never in his life had the burglar come across such a weird, silent dog. Anyway, the man continued with his task, and the dog followed him as though to keep tabs on the total loss of property. Finally, the burglar left, and as soon as he stepped outside the front gate, the dog began barking loudly. Spooked by the peculiar dog, the burglar ran away as swiftly as he could.

Later, Maria asked Chandippatti, 'Why didn't you bark at the thief?'

'The rule is that we should bark at strangers,' Chandippatti responded. 'He is not a stranger. I see him every day. I know him well.'

After this incident, Geevarghese decided that the house needed a better guard dog, one that was smarter and more capable than Chandippatti. One day, he came home leading a dog that looked as ferocious as Hidumban from the Mahabharatham. Hidumban announced his ferociousness by barking all along the way, but as soon as he was at the front gate of Kottarathil Veedu, Chandippatti confronted him. Geevarghese would describe what transpired after thus:

'Chandi just stood there staring into Hidumban's eyes, and Hidumban began to slink back slowly and hid behind me. Next thing you know, the dog broke free of the leash and took off. No one has seen him since! Chandippatti barked and lunged at me for a while. I was so shocked I didn't say anything!'

'Why did you bark at Appachan?' Maria asked Chandippatti.

'As long as I live, the only dog in this house will be me,' Chandippatti told her. 'I was just letting him know that.'

That, in essence, was Chandippatti. He did not bark at the eagles who snatched the chickens or at the strangers who entered the compound. He only barked when he felt like it, and then he barked to his heart's content.

Finally, fed up with Chandippatti's arrogant self-regard, Mariyamma decided to banish him. One day, when the jeep taking rubber sheets to the market set out from Kottarathil Veedu, Mariyamma loaded Chandippatti in the back. She was worried that he would bark and alert Maria, but Chandippatti climbed in willingly and silently.

'Left from the Kottarathil compound, and then right at the junction. Down the road to the Church of Geevarghese Sahada. Right turn. Landmarks on the road: a house with a cement boat on top of it, a poster of the film *Santha Oru Devatha*, a toddy shop. Well, can't depend on the toddy shop because they are everywhere. Past the side of the toddy shop, a veterinary hospital and a house with a red jeep parked in the yard. Left turn, and onwards to the signboard 'Jumbo Circus'. Straight down the road, and there's the market.'

When they got to the market, the driver quickly let Chandippatti out of the jeep and disappeared.

On seeing a strange new dog in the area, the market dogs came ready to attack, but they were humbled before Chandippatti's preternatural intelligence. Soon, Chandippatti became the unquestioned leader of all the dogs in the area. They took him offerings of the tastiest meal to be had – meat, rotten to perfection! Desperate to bear his children, local bitches scurried after him, and Chandippatti established a queue system to deal with the crowd. But when those who had their turn began to wait at the back of the queue hoping for a second turn, Chandippatti put an end to the entire enterprise.

Before long, Chandippatti's gang of mongrels became the stuff of nightmares for all creatures, from moths to humans, in and around the market area. Intrigued by the gang, a white sahib followed them everywhere. Eventually, he secured a scholarship for the study of Indian street dogs and became well known through his participation on TV panel-shows.

One time, when the prime minister made a visit, the notorious gang took over the meeting ground. The meeting had to be abandoned and the prime minister moved to a safe location under strict security measures. Another time, a week-long tourism festival had to be cancelled after the gang defecated all along the royal street where it was to take place and covered it with their appi. People in Kottarathil Veedu and their neighbours read about these incidents in the newspapers, but it never occurred to them that it was their very own Chandippatti who was behind all these shenanigans.

Finally, the city corporation had to do something, and dog catchers began to rush hither and thither in their vehicles. As the atmosphere turned tense, Chandippatti recalled Kottarathil Veedu and the landmarks that would help him find his way back.

When he got to Jumbo Circus, Chandippatti made new friends: a lion who claimed to be the king of the forest even though he had never seen a forest; an intelligent parrot who had no inkling of his own intelligence; a dog of a foreign breed who, although snooty at first, soon accepted Chandippatti's dominance; a tiger who promised to visit Chandippatti at Kottarathil Veedu soon…

As he retraced his way home, Chandippatti was confused at times. Having been driven elsewhere by its owner, the red jeep was not where it was supposed to be, and when it dawned on him that a jeep, after all, was a thing that was supposed to move around, Chandippatti was embarrassed at his foolishness. The fact that the *Santha Oru Devatha* film poster had been replaced with one for *Shalini Ente Koottukaari* only added to his confusion.

Anyway, the Chandippatti who returned to Kottarathil Veedu was someone who could run on his hind legs, walk steadily backwards, kick a football with his fore legs, and dance the twist shaking his bum like the heroines in Hindi films.

Maria, ecstatic that Chandippatti had returned, gave him a plateful of chicken curry but he turned his nose up at it. He told her about the tasty meat he used to feast on at the market. He also told her about the imminent visit of the tiger, and Maria waited eagerly for the day until, as time passed, she forgot all about it. Mariyamma's hatred for Chandippatti had only increased, but she did not try to banish him again.

With the exception of Maria, everyone in Kottarathil Veedu thought of Geevarghese as a terrible person. For Sheena, Thomachan and Maria's mama, Anna, the biggest sorrow of their lives was that he was their father. Geevarghese spent most of his time in the toddy shop, making everyone wonder how a man born into such a good family had ended up like that. But outside of his home, Geevarghese was a happy, jolly man. 'I don't know, the home atmosphere and I don't seem to agree with each other,' he would say, and by 'home' he meant not just his own home but homes in general.

So, these were Little Maria's friends and companions: a grandfather, Geevarghese, who spent most of his time in toddy shops and gallivanting around the village, taking his granddaughter along; a great-grandfather, Kuncheriya valyappachan, who was over ninety years old and at death's door; a great aunt, Anna valyamma, who was in the grip of dementia; an ancestor, Chirammel Kathanar, who was a priest and had died generations ago; other dead family members, including Mathiri valyammachi, from the stories her grandfather told her; and Chandippatti, a dog who philosophized non-stop. Was it any wonder that Maria turned out the way she did!

This did not mean that there were no normal people in Kottarathil Veedu. It would be impossible to find another person as normal as Mariyamma, her grandmother, in the whole wide world. The only abnormal thing Mariyamma had ever done was to laugh uncontrollably, for almost an hour, when her mother-in-law had once asked her what she was going to cook for the evening meal. That was the one hour when Geevarghese felt the deepest love for her, the one hour that he remembered nostalgically when he thought of their whole life together.

Then there was Sheena. A history teacher and a staunch supporter of communism, her biggest desire was to become a Naxalite. But, realizing that her father would break her legs if she became one, she had nipped that desire in the bud. She was in love with a colleague at the college where she taught. Knowing that 'love' was another thing that would prompt her father to break her legs, she had tried her hardest to nip that, too, in the bud. But, as we all know, this was not an easy task. Often, in the night, Sheena hugged Maria and sobbed over the destiny of her love. She was a college teacher, granted, but she had a tender heart. She was of the acceptable age for marriage. In those days, it was hard enough finding a husband for a working woman with a bit of education, so imagine finding one for someone who had an MA degree and taught in a college! And when they did find prospective matches after searching all over the place, Sheena found some random reason to send them packing. Mariyamma was a bundle of worries about this, especially as her drunkard of a husband couldn't be bothered.

Finally, when a proposal came from a man named Mathayi, try as she might, Sheena could not find an excuse to refuse him. He, too, had an MA degree and worked as a manager in a public sector bank. He was an only son from an enormously wealthy family. When it looked as though the marriage might go ahead, Sheena presented her objection before Mariyamma: she could not even entertain the thought of marrying someone whose name was Mathayi. Mariyamma responded with a resounding slap on her cheek which sent Sheena reeling to the floor, but she held her ground – she would not marry a man named Mathayi.

Mathayi had fallen for Sheena from the moment he set eyes on her, and so was deeply hurt by her rejection. And when the marriage broker told him the reason, he fell into a depression. In the end, he found some solace by formally changing his name from Mathayi to the more fashionable Mathew. But you know how our people are ... they just continued calling him Mathayi.

Jomon, Sheena's lover, was, all things considered, a good match for her. He taught in the same college, and although not from a family as prominent or wealthy as Kottarathil Veedu, he too was a Syrian Christian. And since he had a good job, his family's financial status was not that important. Above all, he had a name that was fashionable in those days. There was the fact that he was fifteen years older than Sheena, but if she did not find that to be a problem, why should it worry anyone else?

When Sheena found a way to scupper the match with Mathayi, Geevarghese got involved. 'Enough of your college and teaching,' he said, and locked her up in a room. One week later, Jomon came to Kottarathil Veedu and asked Geevarghese for Sheena's hand in marriage. Geevarghese responded by calling him all kinds of names, but Jomon told him, calmly and quietly, that he would go to the police and file a habeas corpus petition. That scared Geevarghese because, like everyone else in the country, he too was afraid of the police ever since the Emergency. And on top of that, the threat of a court case and words like 'habeas corpus'! Even after they got married, the thought of 'habeas corpus' would make Geevarghese anxious whenever he was in Jomon's presence. But those were things that would happen after Maria left Kottarathil Veedu.

The other inhabitant of Kottarathil Veedu who was entirely normal was the youngest of Geevarghese and Mariyamma's children, Shajan – Little Maria's Shajan chachan – who was studying medicine. When he came home on holidays, Maria would take his stethoscope and run to Chandippatti. 'Take a deep breath,' she would say to him. This was one of Chandippatti's favourite games. Shajan chachan, Maria and Chandippatti would get into the Impala car and go for a drive. Shajan chachan would take them to Swamy's bakery in the city and buy Joy ice cream for Maria and Parle Gluco biscuits for Chandippatti. Chandi tried telling him several times that he would rather have the ice cream, but for some reason Shajan never understood. Like Maria, Chandi too called him Shajan chachan.

By the time Maria grew up, Joy ice cream had almost disappeared. Once, when she was gripped by a desire to eat it, Aravind travelled all over the district looking for a shop that stocked it. And when he finally found a place, poor Aravind ordered all the flavours. Watching Maria's joy, he felt that if he died right there and then, he would die contented.

'This doesn't taste as good as it used to,' Maria said after eating a couple of spoons. 'Come, let's go.'

That was the day Aravind named her the 'Cat with the Bad Attitude'.

The Cat with the Bad Attitude was a character from a Russian folk tale. A little girl drew a picture of a cat. A single cat, all on its own.

'I'll need a house to live in, won't I?' the cat asked the girl.

A fair question, the girl felt, so she drew a house.

'What about a garden for me to play in?' asked the cat.

The girl drew a garden.

'And a chair for me to curl up and sleep in?'

The girl drew a chair.

'A fire to keep me warm?'

The girl drew a hearth and a fire.

'And birds and butterflies to chase in the garden?'

By now, the girl was beginning to get pissed off, but she drew them anyway. And just as she finished, out came the next demand.

'What about a window for me to come and go?'

Cursing herself for drawing the cat in the first place, the girl drew a window.

'I don't like this house,' said the cat, and walked out through the window.

That was the story of the Cat with the Bad Attitude.

Even as a student, when Shajan was home for vacation, people came to Kottarathil Veedu with all kinds of ailments. He treated most of them, sending only the ones he could not deal with to the hospital in the city. When he treated his patients, Little Maria stood by as his helper, and Chandippatti as her helper. During one such vacation time, Sumathi brought her son, Kuttappayi, who was burning up with fever, to Shajan. When Shajan went to get the medicine, Little Maria lay down next to the boy and hugged his hot body tightly. Poor Kuttappayi … in an almost unconscious state with the fever, he did not even realize that he was experiencing the first embrace of love in his life.

You know there are some people who experience the pain of those around them intensely? Shajan was one of them. After he finished his studies, Shajan took a job at a charitable hospital in one of the most deprived areas in the district. He married a woman from a poor family, not out of love but with the sole purpose of helping her into a better life. Geevarghese fell out with him because of this decision. Of all his twelve children, Shajan was the only one Geevarghese had a special bond with. Shajan's empathy towards his fellow human beings who were less fortunate touched him. Shajan, too, was very fond of his father despite his waywardness and his drinking habit. The marriage severed this bond. Geevarghese ordered him to leave the house if he wished to do as he pleased, and Shajan retorted that he would never come back to Kottarathil Veedu. Still, when it was time to divide the house and the property between his offspring, Geevarghese followed custom and set aside Kottarathil Veedu for his youngest son, Shajan.

It was an old Syrian Christian house, built by Mathu, the father of Geevarghese's father Kuncheriya, and rebuilt later by Kuncheriya. Every room in the house had bedsteads and tables and almirahs with intricate carvings – furniture that is known these days as 'antique'. The ninety-year-old Kuncheriya continued to live amidst them as though he was another antique piece.

Even at that age, Kuncheriya was in good condition. His breakfast consisted of five or six appams or one and a half lengths of puttu or a couple of plates of pidi with a big plate of meat curry, accompanied by a glass of milk and a steamed ethappazham. He woke up early to do his morning rituals. Kuncheriya did not go to the toilet; he 'went out'. There were several toilets in the house, but Kuncheriya could accomplish his deed only if he sat out in the open. In any case, most people did that in those days. Kuncheriya hated bathing and did not understand why people had a bath every day; he was convinced he was quite clean without it. Whenever he complained about his son's unclean soul, Geevarghese would retaliate: 'That is as may be, but you stink!'

Kuncheriya spent the time between his morning and midday meals sitting on an easy chair, reading the Bible and looking over the next month's projected income. At 10 a.m., Anna would bring him another steamed ethappazham and a glass of coffee, made only with milk and no water, the one task she did without fail despite the dementia that affected her memory. For his lunch, Kuncheriya would have two plates of rice with roasted buffalo meat, chicken curry, fried fish and fish koottan, rounding off the meal with a few small bananas.

'The old man won't die until he attends his grandchildren's funerals,' Geevarghese would tell Maria. 'And he'll walk all the way to the graveyard!'

Geevarghese's unchristian ways enraged Kuncheriya. 'The only consolation I have is that I won't have to see this bastard after I die,' he would say. 'Hell is where he's headed.' Despite his advanced age, it was Kuncheriya who controlled the finances of the household, denying Geevarghese free access to money to squander and to spend in the toddy shops. So, at the age of sixty-six, he still stole from his father's money box every time he had a chance.

'I am really against stealing,' Geevarghese told Maria, 'but I don't have any other option.'

And to declare her solidarity with her grandfather, Maria too began stealing until Neena caught her red-handed.

'Get yourself a special coffin made,' Geevarghese told Kuncheriya, fed up. 'One with pockets to take all your money with you.'

'I am not taking it with me, but I won't give a single paisa to you,' Kuncheriya retorted. 'When I get to heaven, I have Karthaveeshomishiha to take care of my every need.'

Maria, having overheard the conversation, dreamt of Karthav Eesho Mishiha taking Kuncheriya a glass of lemonade on a tray and standing around chatting with him as he drank it.

Whenever the argument between father and son got serious, Geevarghese would command Kuncheriya to leave the house. Sometimes, Kuncheriya took it as a challenge and went to his daughter's house nearby. At other times, he ignored Geevarghese, saying that the house was rightfully his and that it was Geevarghese who must leave. In return, Geevarghese called his father all the obscene words he knew, and Kuncheriya responded in kind, but anyone listening to the exchange would think he was reading from the Bible.

If, as a result of the argument, Kuncheriya went to his daughter's house, it only riled up Geevarghese further. Within a couple of days, he would set out to bring his father back, and Kuncheriya would follow him home silently. And if his son did not come to fetch him, Kuncheriya would return anyway after a couple of days, and quietly sit on an easy chair on the veranda while Geevarghese sat on the other easy chair as though nothing important had happened.

As time passed, Geevarghese realized that his father was never going to loosen his grip on the family wealth, and he began to think that his father would outlive him. So, with the express purpose of making some money for his everyday expenses, he opened a miscellaneous store at the junction.

'No one from this family will become a shopkeeper,' Kuncheriya roared, banging his walking stick on the ground. 'That too a useless shop like this!'

In truth, the income from the shop was barely enough for Geevarghese's needs, but he liked his new enterprise. 'It's good to be engaged in something,' he told Maria. The Parry's sweet in its green wrapper and the Nutrine in its orange wrapper, available only in Geevarghese's shop, were highly tempting for the local children. But since he entertained only ready-cash transactions, and the children usually had not a single paisa in their pockets, they kept their distance and continued enjoying the chakkaramittayi and teeth-shattering kattimittayi that could be bought in other shops for four cashew nuts or six areca nuts. Maria was the chief consumer of the sweets and snacks in Geevarghese's shop. She bought the sweets, took out the exact amount from the cash box and gave it to Geevarghese, and he took the money from her and put it back in the cash box.

Too busy with his other concerns, Geevarghese soon appointed a helper at the shop. 'That bastard Josootty is eating us out of house and home,' bellowed Kuncheriya.

The primary audience for Kuncheriya's complaints was Mariyamma. She was fifteen years old when she had come to Kottarathil Veedu as Geevarghese's bride. In the long years of marriage that followed, she gave birth to fifteen children. Other than the two who had died as infants, and a son who everyone had expected would grow up to be a saint but was called back by the Lord at the age of twelve, the rest of her children led good lives in this world.

Many years later, Maria would ask Mariyamma: 'Ammachi, how is it possible to give birth to so many children? Could you not have stopped and thought about it for a minute?'

'This is not something you do after thinking about it,' Mariyamma would reply, her voice replete with resentment and anger against the whole world. 'Besides, who has the time to think in the middle of all these childbirths?'

Having been born into a God-fearing Christian family, Mariyamma was not able to adjust to married life even after years had passed. She thought initially that Geevarghese was in the grip of Satan, but eventually came to wonder whether he was Satan himself. Geevarghese was who he was even as a young lad, but his mother, Shoshamma, blamed Mariyamma for his bad behaviour, an accusation that led to a pitched battle between the two that lasted until Shoshamma's death.

Speaking of Shoshamma's death ... that was a funny incident. She and Anna had just returned from the funeral of the priest, Thomman Kathanar.

'As God is my witness ... died just like that, didn't he, for no reason at all? Anna, you remember, even yesterday he conducted the Qurbana as usual. Who'd have thought he'd go like this!'

'That's just how it is, Chedathi. Some people don't need any reason to leave this world. Karthav decides it is time, and that's that! Mattathil Thankamma ... now, didn't she go just like that as she was laughing at something? Didn't even have the time to finish laughing! You remember.'

'Still. To die so suddenly like that ... Fetch me a glass of kanjivellam, Anna. I'm very tired from walking all that way.'

Shoshamma sat down on a chair, and by the time Anna came back with the kanjivellam, she was dead.

Mariyamma's only solace in her husband's house was Kuncheriya. He worshipped the daughter-in-law who had entered his house all those years ago with a face that resembled the Virgin Mother and a picture of Geevarghese Sahada, St George the Martyr, who was the patron saint of the land.

Shoshamma's object of worship was her son, Geevarghese.

'Granted he is a bit mischievous, but look at that face! Such divinity! Our Karthaveeshomishiha knew exactly what He was doing when He made him mischievous, because otherwise our one and only son would have gone off to become a great saint!'

And when he stole money from Kuncheriya, she said, 'He is just having a bit of fun!'

'Children turn out bad because of their mothers,' Geevarghese would tell Maria many years later. 'It's the way of the world.'

Mariyamma's culinary skills were as famous as her beauty, but Geevarghese ate at home only on rare occasions. 'I don't know what it is,' he would say, 'but the food at home does not seem to agree with me.' Here too, by 'home' he meant not just his home but the idea of home itself. Be that as it may, the person who got the opportunity to enjoy Mariyamma's culinary skills and her beauty was Mathachan, the son of Kuncheriya's dead younger brother, Paulo.

When he sat down at the table and Mariyamma served him pidi and meat curry, Mathachan considered himself to be a lucky man. Much luckier than Geevarghese.

'Do you know the secret behind tasty food?' he would ask Mariyamma, making sure that no one else was around. 'It's prepared with an added ingredient – love.'

He would steal a glance at her, hoping to see the beautiful smile on her beautiful face. Was there a hidden meaning behind that smile? He would never know. But he found consolation in the fact that the smile was absent when Geevarghese was around. He did not know what to call the feeling he had for Mariyamma. The phrase 'platonic love' was not in circulation in those days.

Within the first year of their marriage, Mariyamma gave birth to their first child. Mariyamma's relatives said that the infant looked like her while Geevarghese's relatives insisted that she looked like him. Geevarghese was amazed at the fact that he felt no special emotion when he looked at the child, his own flesh and blood. And when everyone exclaimed over the child's beauty, he scrutinized it from various angles but failed to see what they saw. Mariyamma was shocked to realize that Geevarghese had no tender feeling even towards his own child. When she was pregnant, she had secretly nursed the hope that the child they had created together would help seal some sort of bond between them. Eventually, she resigned herself to accepting the fact that her husband was an animal devoid of humanly emotions.

The disinterest he felt for his firstborn did not dissuade Geevarghese from making more babies with Mariyamma. 'Whether I like it or not, they keep on coming anyway,' he said.

'Forget about him, my dear,' Kuncheriya told Mariyamma. 'You must make sure you give them their father's love too.'

Geevarghese led a busy life, so it was Kuncheriya who took on the responsibility of registering the children, as they came of age, at the school, paid their fees, and placed his signature – a little cross enclosed in a circle – on the necessary documents. It was only after their firstborn, Susanna, finished Class 10 that Geevarghese realized his daughter was not named Susanna Geevarghese as was the custom but Susanna Kuncheriya. A man like Geevarghese should not have been affected by this fact, but he was upset.

'Bastard got me!' he said, gazing at his father innocently munching on an appam.

And not just the one time! Susanna Kuncheriya, Zakariya Kuncheriya, Anna Kuncheriya, John Kuncheriya, Paul Kuncheriya, Mary Kuncheriya, Daisy Kuncheriya, Babu Kuncheriya, Ramani Kuncheriya, Sheena Kuncheriya, Thomas Kuncheriya, Neena Kuncheriya – he got him twelve times! As Geevarghese stood there, hurt and with overflowing eyes, he glanced outside and saw his youngest son, two and a half years old, playing in the yard. He grabbed him, carried him off to the school and got him registered. In those days, one did not have to wait till the month of June for registering new students at the school. The child wailed loudly as his father was a stranger to him. Still, because of this reflex action, Geevarghese's youngest son Shajan – the one who would become a doctor – became Shajan Geevarghese.

Kuncheriya had to resort to these underhand tactics to express his anger towards Geevarghese.

'Explain this to me, Anna. I don't understand why he is so angry at my son,' Shoshamma said. 'My boy doesn't come home often because of *her*, Mariyamma. He never used to drink this much before he was married, don't you remember?'

'Of course, I do,' Anna replied between mouthfuls of puttu and fish curry. 'I think Geevarghese is the best and most well behaved of all the young men in this area. Well, he does like to roam around, but young men should do that. Not sit in the kitchen all the time like Mathachan. And that too, in someone else's kitchen!'

'Oh, Anna! Mathachan and Mariyamma – do they have to spend so much time together? What will people say? I am worried that the servants have already started whispering about it.'

'Well ... I'm not sure it's the fault of anyone in particular, Chedathi,' Anna said. 'Geevarghese who should be at home is always out, and Mathachan who should be out is always in. That's the problem.'

Anna was from a distant, impoverished branch of the Kottarathil family, and had come to live in Kottarathil Veedu even before Shoshamma married Kuncheriya. It was Kuncheriya's mother Mathiri – famous all around as Mathiri the Proclaimer – who gave Anna asylum in Kottarathil Veedu. She grew up alongside Kuncheriya and Paulo, happily enjoying her life, until Kuncheriya got married and Shoshamma arrived as his bride. Anna thought of herself as a member of the family, but Shoshamma corrected her every time this happened – 'Someone who looks after the household, that is all,' she would remind Anna whenever she had a chance. So, it was among the servants and the workers in the orchards that Anna used her position and power as a member of the family.

'Don't you servants concern yourself with what's happening in the household,' Anna would declare. 'We, the family members, are here to take care of that, and if any of you outsiders have anything to say, I will not tolerate it.'

Years later, when Mariyamma watched her mega serials on TV, Geevarghese would remember Anna. All mega serials began with an Anna.

What Anna felt for Shoshamma was jealousy combined with hatred. The big house ... the endless wealth ... the numerous servants ... the husband who gave her all this ... Anna hated Shoshamma for it all. It would be so nice to have a good husband, and she sighed over it. She did not sigh over the house, the wealth or the servants, because all of that came with the husband. When she thought of her hatred for Shoshamma, who was also her benefactor, she consoled herself, saying, 'Shoshamma chedathi is not an easy person to love.' For her own survival, she pretended to love Shoshamma deeply, and as time passed, she was unsure what she felt towards Shoshamma.

As a young woman, Anna had been stunningly beautiful. Wasted beauty, according to Geevarghese. Anna never knew a man but, right from her youth, she knew her own body. She partook in its pleasures, immersed herself in its possibilities, with a passion that a man could never have satisfied. For Anna, her body was an instrument that would take her to the heights of intoxication. In its depths, she came to know a level of joy that women like Mathiri, Shoshamma, Mariyamma and a million others who had known men would never experience. But, for the world outside, Anna was a stupid woman, a slow and clueless woman, a woman who spent all her time eating something or the other.

Whenever Mathiri ran into Anna, she smiled at her, and Anna began to feel that it was a smile pregnant with meaning, and she tried to avoid Mathiri in order to avoid being smiled at that way. But Mathiri did not mean anything by her smile. She smiled at Anna in the same way she smiled at their cow Velumbi, their parrot Ammini, and her grandsons Geevarghese and Mathachan. One day, as Anna was scraping coconut, Mathiri, who did not usually enter the kitchen, came in. Anna tried to avoid making eye contact, but Mathiri smiled at her, and as usual, the smile disconcerted Anna.

'Why are you smiling?' she asked, taking her courage in her hands.

'Isn't it nice to smile?' Mathiri asked in return.

'But why are you smiling like this?'

The question made Mathiri laugh loudly and without stopping. It only made Anna more confused, and in her consternation, she slipped off the chirava – the wooden coconut scraper stool – and fell on the floor. This sent Mathiri into another paroxysm of laughter. She laughed until her stomach hurt, and yet she continued laughing.

Somewhere along the way, Kuncheriya wanted to get Anna married off, but Shoshamma persuaded him otherwise, saying that Kottarathil Veedu was the best place for an orphan like Anna until, gradually, he forgot about it. Yet, whenever he saw Anna, he felt there was something about her that he had forgotten and tried to recall what it was. Much later, when he was ninety-five years old, as he sat having his breakfast one day, he would recall, out of the blue, what it was that he had forgotten. By then, Anna would have been dead for many years.

Geevarghese spent his days in the toddy shops and with the servants, especially with Kali. Kali was his weakness, indeed the weakness of the entire area. Kali sent the customs and rules of the land flying in the wind, slept with any man she fancied despite having a husband, lay down by the wayside after drinking toddy with Geevarghese and Kelan and Velayudhan. She, too, felt a deep love for Geevarghese, not a simple love that a woman felt for a man, but the specific love that Kali felt for Geevarghese. And despite this abiding love within her, she slept with other men.

One day, Kali, Geevarghese and Velayudhan sat drinking toddy in a corner of Kuncheriya's compound. Kali had a handful of cashew nuts – roasted and to be roasted – tucked in the waist-fold of her mundu. In her inebriated state, she took out an unroasted cashew nut and buried it in the soil.

'Eda, Geevarghese nanaarey, here you go,' she said. 'A cashew tree for you from me.'

It would be on the branches of the cashew tree that sprouted from the seed Kali planted on that day that, years later, Little Maria would play 'bus driving' and sit waiting for Kuttappayi, where a grown-up Maria would see Kuttappayi after a gap of many years. But these were events yet to happen.

When Kali was Kali, she called Geevarghese 'nanaarey' – boss man – and when she was Drunken Kali, she prefixed it with the disrespectful 'eda'. Geevarghese was happy either way. Velayudhan looked lustfully at Kali as she sat hunched over the seed she was planting. He had always lusted after her, but Kali refused to sleep with him. Velayudhan was – how to put it – a njanugapununga. Gormless.

Thimman, a hawker, came across them as they sat there. He was from a seaside village but wandered around inland selling odds and ends. He was lost in his thoughts – 'How long have I been wandering around like this! How long has it been since I've had a chance to talk to someone other than to ask them "do you want this" or "what about that". What sort of life is this!' He longed to have a heart to heart with someone, and that was when he came across Geevarghese and his friends.

No one asked him anything, but Thimman began to tell them about the sea, about his hut by the seashore, about his friends who went deep-sea fishing. He told them that he had become a hawker and not a fisherman because he suffered from seasickness. He did not tell them anything about his life because there was nothing worth telling, and continued talking about the sea instead.

His people did not know what lay beyond the sea. The sea was their God, he said, so they assumed that heaven was what lay on the other side of it. A man, the most courageous and knowledgeable among his people, had set out to find what lay beyond, but he had not returned yet. Thimman's folk assumed that he was still searching.

A desire to see the sea surged up within Geevarghese. He had heard about the sea – Karthav Eesho Mishiha had disciples who had gone fishing in the sea, and Karthav Himself had walked on the sea. 'Shall we go see the sea?' Geevarghese asked Kali and Velayudhan. Kali scrambled up immediately because she, too, wanted to see the sea, and because it was Geevarghese who was asking. But Velayudhan declined, suddenly finding an unbearable pain in his knees. He did not care about the sea; he cared only about getting drunk.

When Kali and Geevarghese reached the seashore after two whole days of walking, the sun was all set to dive into the sea. As he stood there with his arm around Kali's waist, watching the endless expanse of the blue water and the red sun about to drown in it, Geevarghese had an epiphany. It was not about the universe or about the sea, but about the fact that he should have married Kali and not Mariyamma. Still, the Geevarghese who had seen the sea was a different man from the Geevarghese who had not seen the sea. The depth, the expanse, and most importantly, the profound sense of mystery of the sea changed him. He would not see the sea ever again in his life, not because he did not have the opportunity but because, if he were to see the sea again, the experience of 'seeing the sea' that he had just had would become meaningless.

On the Sunday after he returned from the sea, Geevarghese went to church for the Qurbana. The priest's sermon on the day was on the topic 'Non-Christians Are Bound for Hell'. Geevarghese listened for a few minutes, and then stood up.

'If that were the case, the first person to go to hell would have been Karthaveeshomishiha, right? He was a Jew after all, wasn't he?' he said. 'Don't let me hear you talk nonsense like this again or I'll break your knees. Don't worry yourself about matters that don't concern you, just do the Qurbana and piss off.'

When they got together to drink toddy, Geevarghese told Kelan, Velayudhan and Kali not to call him 'nanaarey' any more. Kelan embraced him happily while Velayudhan stared at him as though he had gone mad. 'Get lost, nanaarey!' Kali said, laughing, and they all continued calling him 'nanaarey'. It was difficult to change age-old habits.

People do not become enlightened because of a single incident. It requires several important factors such as birth, life up until the time of enlightenment, the acquiring of knowledge, and so on. So, even though Geevarghese experienced enlightenment, it was his unenlightened side that was predominant, and because of that he continued his childish habits such as eating sugar and eavesdropping whenever someone told the children stories.

A few days after they had returned from the sea, Kali eloped with Thimman. The sea had made such a strong impression on her. And with Kali gone, Geevarghese discarded the little enlightenment he had acquired and became a full-time drunk.

Well, what was a man to do when there was so much toddy all around? 'We can't let it go to waste, can we?' he asked. 'My appan used to drink too, did you know? Then, one day, Geevarghese Sahada came to him in a dream and asked him to stop. That's when he gave up drinking.'

Much later, Maria would ask Mariyamma about the truth of this story.

'Do not speak nonsense about that saintly soul,' Mariyamma said with a serious expression that verged on the comical.

Maria assumed that by 'saintly soul' she meant Geevarghese Sahada, but Mariyamma was referring to Kuncheriya. After all, given that Geevarghese Sahada was an actual saint, there was no need to refer to him specifically as a saintly soul.

# 5

# The Sorrows of Geevarghese Sahada

Geevarghese Sahada, St George the Martyr, was the beloved punyalachan – patron saint – of the land. His primary job was to protect the land's chickens from foxes, eagles and snakes – especially from snakes. There was a story that he had, once upon a time, killed a snake, so everyone assumed he was the sworn enemy of all snakes. As they were not acquainted with dragons, they took the fearsome creature in the pictures of Geevarghese Sahada to be a type of snake, and obviously it became his duty to protect the chickens from the snakes. As time went by, people updated the things they expected him to protect the chickens from, and added the fox, the eagle and the wildcat called kaattumakkan to the list.

Even a whiff of something untoward near the chicken coops would set matriarchs such as Shoshamma, Mariyamma, Annamma, Pennamma, Thresyamma and others calling out: 'O Punyalacha, protect my chickens…'

Geevarghese Sahada heeded their call and protected the chickens, except on the occasions when he was in a contrary mood. Then he ignored them completely.

'I know they mean well and all, but come on! Do they think I have nothing else to do except look after their chickens? What foolishness!'

And for all that, did a single person in the land bother to find out what was going on with Geevarghese Sahada? No. Truth be told, Geevarghese Sahada was bored stiff. He had been sitting at the same spot for as long as he could remember, looking out at the same scenery, seeing the same people ... No one even seemed to remember that he was once a soldier who had fought in so many wars, seen so many sights. Then there was the awkward way in which he was made to sit – straddled on a horse, aiming his spear at the snake at its feet. The spear was within an inch of the snake, but try as he might, it never made actual contact with the creature. And this land! Barely the size of a paisa! So, obviously Geevarghese Sahada was bored.

Besides, the punyalachan was a sentimental type. It hurt him that the people of the land never really thought about him. He was envious of the patron saints of other nations, and sighed deeply when he thought of their good fortune.

'I take care of all these people and their chickens. Yet, does a single one of them think about me? Wonder how I am doing? I know what's inside each one of them. I watch over them even when they're asleep. I don't mind helping them, but when I see their attitude ... it makes me so mad! Do they ever think that I, too, have a heart?'

That was the real issue – Geevarghese Sahada, too, had a heart.

'Does any other punyalachan care about his wards as much as I do? People here live up to a hundred and ten! And in all that time, do they have to face any real problems? They haven't even heard about earthquakes and volcanoes or lived through a war. The number of wars I have fought in … These people don't even know what a real war is!'

His people's complete disregard for his welfare turned Geevarghese Sahada's tender heart to thoughts of revenge. He was certain about one thing – whatever the mode of exacting revenge, it should be entertaining. His initial thought was to make them fight with one another, but he discarded this idea for two reasons:

1) Pitting people against each other was an old method of revenge that had been used by many before, and Geevarghese Sahada wanted a brand-new method.
2) All said and done, Geevarghese Sahada still loved his people.

Finally, after considering and discarding several ideas, Geevarghese Sahada settled on one: he would enter their dreams.

That morning, when he got up, Geevarghese found himself in the grip of a nameless fear. He had spent the previous day like any other, and had returned home from the toddy shop after midnight, along the way rewarding a mongrel bitch with a kick. Had he run into Mariyamma? He could not remember. But, that night…

'You're not afraid of me, are you?'

'Geevarghese Sahada!'

'Answer me. Are you afraid of me or not?'

'No … Why? Should I be?'

'Most certainly! I am the patron saint of this land. Besides, they have given you my name!'

'Well, I've never felt afraid of you. Felt sorry for you though…'

'For what?'

'The way you sit on that horse! So uncomfortable … and for so long!'

Geevarghese Sahada felt his eyes welling up with tears. At least one person had been worrying about him.

'Geevarghese, you must stop all this nonsense and live a proper life. I've come to tell you this.'

'I've no intention of doing any such thing.'

'Well, we'll see, won't we?' said Geevarghese Sahada and disappeared.

Geevarghese spent the rest of the night tossing and turning in his sleep. The answers he had given to Geevarghese Sahada's questions were not the ones that were in his mind. He did not intend to disrespect the saint, but what to do, it was a dream after all, and we don't really have much control over our dreams. So, the answers that came out of his mouth were the exact opposite of what he had intended to say.

As his restless sleep progressed, Geevarghese Sahada reappeared in Geevarghese's dream. He was seated on an elephant this time. The horse, his traditional ride, was an animal unfamiliar to the region, which was probably why he had exchanged it for an elephant. A kind of local adaptation. Sitting on top of the elephant, Geevarghese Sahada began chasing Geevarghese, and all night in his sleep Geevarghese ran until he was fed up.

After that, night after night, Geevarghese began to have the same dream. The same questions, the same answers, and the same elephant…

'Can't he occasionally come up with something new?' Geevarghese thought dejectedly.

Meanwhile, Mariyamma began to have dreams about Geevarghese Sahada following her with a rose in his hand. It made her feel guilty and she began thinking about hell.

Soon, everyone in the land began to see the punyalachan in their dreams. There was a problem with these dreams though. They lacked variety or – how to put it – a certain artistry. In fairness, Geevarghese Sahada's world had been confined to this one region for so many years, thus restricting his experiential knowledge. The children of the land dreamt that Geevarghese Sahada played kuttiyum-kolum with them. Thresya had a dream that Geevarghese Sahada pushed her cow into the well. Again, let's be fair, when the cow had a bit of a turn once, Thresya had promised an offering to Geevarghese Sahada, but then reneged after it got well, convincing herself that it wasn't a big deal after all. She had forgotten all about it and had assumed that Geevarghese Sahada would not have taken this silly matter so seriously.

Geevarghese Sahada entered the parish priest Thomman Kathanar's dreams and began giving him tips about how to make the Qurbana more interesting. Eventually, fed up with Geevarghese Sahada's insistence, the priest lost all interest in offering the Qurbana.

Gradually, everyone had had enough of Geevarghese Sahada. When they saw him during the day, they began to worry about their nightly sleep, and eventually, in order to avoid seeing him, they stopped going to the church.

That only increased Geevarghese Sahada's sorrows.

Geevarghese Sahada decided to take a break, and one night, without warning, he disappeared from people's dreams. He had set out on a world tour.

As he explored the world, Geevarghese Sahada also used his time to learn about the management styles of other patron saints.

But it is safe to assume that this plan was not entirely successful because the other patron saints were still figuring out the confused place the world had become at the end of the world war. Besides, it was a time of great economic setback. Geevarghese Sahada tried to help many of his fellow patron saints, but having had no experience in managing hardship or looking after people who were struggling, he only added to their confusion which, in the end, invited the displeasure of some of them. Undaunted, Geevarghese Sahada continued with his mission.

In the enjoyment of this new venture, Geevarghese Sahada postponed his return several times. And when he returned finally, things were in bad shape. With no one to control them, the foxes and the snakes of the land considered each day a feast day, and the entire land had taken to praying arduously to Geevarghese Sahada. Feeling extremely guilty, he made the hens lay two eggs a day. People were placated and happy again, and they promptly forgot all about the punyalachan.

Geevarghese Sahada began the dreams again, but this time around, they were different. Seeing the world outside had developed his artistry. He also stopped the habit of appearing in people's dreams himself. And since the first world tour had been a resounding success, Geevarghese Sahada made it a regular event. In the days when Geevarghese Sahada was away, the only consolation people had was their dreams.

'There's a land where everyone is equal,' toddy tapper Kelan said to Geevarghese one day. 'A land where one person doesn't have to call another person "nanaarey". I saw it in my dream.'

'You mean a land where you and I are the same?' asked Geevarghese.

'Mm ... a land where no one is below anyone else. If only such a land really existed...'

Kelan would see many other dreams in the days to come, but the thought of this particular dream would always make him nostalgic. Years later, Kelan would become the first communist in the land.

'There's this thing,' Mariyamma told Mathachan in secret. 'Quite sweet ... sweeter than payasam even ... and soft, too, softer than vattayappam!'

'How did you come to know of this thing?' Mathachan asked. Whenever Mathachan looked at Mariyamma, butterflies flitted around his eyes. Butterflies like dreams ... dreams like butterflies...

Mariyamma stood very close to Mathachan in order not to upset the butterflies. 'I had a dream,' she whispered.

Mathachan felt that the statement 'I had a dream' had no connection to what they were talking about, and that if he asked, 'What was it about?' she would answer, 'Butterflies.' But she just smiled her smile and stood there.

Mathachan wanted to look at that smile until the day he died, but Anna entered the kitchen on the pretext of looking for something, and the butterflies flitted away.

'Did you see how it was made?'

'No, but I can still taste it.'

'Then try making it. It might work...'

Mariyamma tried to recall the taste from her dream.

There was the taste of flour...

The taste of milk...

The taste of sugar...

The taste of eggs...

The taste of butter...

And there was the taste of something else...

Mariyamma could not figure out what that something else was. Still, she mixed together flour, milk, sugar, eggs and butter and made 'it'.

'Sweeter than payasam,' said everyone who tasted it. 'Softer than vattayappam…'

'But it's not "it",' Mariyamma said only to Mathachan. 'There's something missing. It was much tastier in the dream.'

Three decades later, Mariyamma would eat cake for the first time in a bakery in town and her eyes would overflow thinking about the dreams … about the butterflies in the dreams … By then, Mathachan would have been dead for many years.

Thus, all the people in the land began to have brand-new, awesome dreams. All, that is, except Geevarghese. Geevarghese Sahada was not ready to forgive Geevarghese, and so Geevarghese continued living his shambolic life, seeing only boring old dreams.

# 6

# Kariyakutty Who Should Have Been a Saint, and Neena Who Became One

'The great thing is that none of us were driven mad from the fear...'

Susanna, Geevarghese's oldest child, would say this many years later. All of Geevarghese's children prayed arduously to Geevarghese Sahada that their father would just up and die. And just in case Geevarghese Sahada found murder distasteful, they added a footnote to their prayers that, at the very least, he would keep their father from coming home in the night.

*Onnanam kunninmel oraadi kunninmel*
*Orayiramkili kooduvechu…*

One night, as he arrived home, Geevarghese's daughter Marykunju, who was in Class 1, sat in front of the kerosene lamp, reading out the poem from the Kerala Padhavali textbook about the one thousand birds that had built their nests on top of the hill, Onnanam Kunnu.

The poem rubbed Geevarghese the wrong way. Not for any particular reason, just that he simply did not like the fact that the birds had built their nests on top of the hill. He dragged the child up and into the barn and commanded her to do a hundred ethams as punishment. It involved holding the right earlobe with the fingers of your left hand, and the left with your right, and bending over and touching the ground with your elbows. When Mariyamma, Kuncheriya and the child's siblings ran into the barn to rescue her, he drew his pocketknife and threatened them to stay away. After she finished the thirty-seventh etham, Marykunju dropped on to a pile of cow dung and fell asleep. Thankfully, by then, Geevarghese had dozed off, so no further harm was done. After making sure that he was truly out for the night by poking his prone body from afar with a long stick, Mariyamma and her children took Marykunju back to the house and washed the cow dung off her body.

The children were careful to stay out of their father's way, making sure that they hid themselves as soon as they saw his shadow. But one day, poor Thomachan was grabbed from behind as he was running away. The moment he realized he had been caught, he fainted from fear. When he came to, Thomachan had changed, and from then on, he would always be listless like a chicken with avian flu.

Geevarghese routinely got his children's names wrong, confusing John with Babu, Babu with Paul, Susanna with Anna, Ramani with Daisy, and so on. The only person he had no confusion about and always called by the right name was Zakariya because, well, it was difficult to be confused about Zakariya.

Zakariya, or Kariyakutty as he was known, was, from a young age, very knowledgeable about all things spiritual. As a child, he did not exhibit a childlike nature and was always engaged in reading the Bible with a sombre expression on his face. In fact, he had been reading the Bible ever since he was able to put letters together to form words. At the age of five, Kuncheriya took him to the school and had him registered, but within two years, the boy dropped out. Listening to the seven-year-old proclaiming, 'The school does not give me anything that nurtures my soul,' Mariyamma fainted and Anna valyamma made the sign of the cross. Geevarghese, meanwhile, was scared of this son of his who went around clutching the Bible, feared him more than Satan himself. 'That boy has a weird look,' he told Kali once. 'It pierces right through me, and guaranteed, I'll be down with a fever for the next week.' His fear was a little exaggerated, but to be fair, there was something truly strange about the boy. When he was eight years old, Kariyakutty put up a little shed in a corner of the yard – just four posts with a few coconut leaves thrown over it as a roof – and began living in it. Inside the shed, he built a platform with mud and planted a wooden crucifix on it. From that day on until his death, Kariyakutty lived in that shed he called 'church'. As for food, all he had was some kanjivellam with a handful of rice in it, once in the morning and once in the night.

It was around this time that Kariyakutty began performing miracles. Nothing major, just a few small ones, like healing Anna valyamma's stomach ache and the excessive bleeding Thankamma, the servant woman who did the outside work, suffered from during her periods. But do not underestimate the importance of these miracles because, remember, Kariyakutty was only eight years old. He had the potential to perform larger, more impressive miracles. Geevarghese declared that the boy was a con artist. But Kariyakutty laid his hand on Anna valyamma's stomach and prayed for a few minutes, and lo and behold, her pain was gone! He was a bit confused as to where to lay his hand when it came to curing Thankamma's ailment, but quickly decided that in her case, too, the stomach was the best location. If Anna valyamma was cured within five minutes, it took almost a day for Thankamma to be cured. Anna valyamma, who was Kariyakutty's most ardent supporter, declared that it took longer with Thankamma because he was not able to lay his hand on the actual afflicted area, and because excessive bleeding, as everyone knows, was a much more serious illness. All that mattered, although it took a bit longer, was that he had healed a months-old illness.

The oldest of the siblings, Susanna, was also devoted to Kariyakutty. She enjoyed being known as the older sister of miracle-performer Kariyakutty, especially since it got rid, at least for a short while, of the label 'the daughter of Geevarghese the Drunk'. Anna, the sibling immediately below Kariyakutty, had no interest in his miracles, or in much else either. His younger brothers – John who was known as Yonankunju and Paul who was called Paulochan – could not stand the sight of him, and the rest of his siblings were too young to understand his handiwork. Many were the times when Yonankunju and Paulochan expressed their displeasure by tearing down Kariyakutty's shed-church. And on each of these occasions, Kariyakutty temporarily forgot his deep-seated spirituality and covered them in blood-curdling abuse as he rebuilt his church.

There were also occasions when the younger brothers' animosity extended beyond damage to property to actual bodily harm. One time, Kariyakutty was sitting peacefully under a cashew tree, immersed in the Holy Bible, when Yonankunju and Paulochan decided that the only place they could play marbles was under that same tree. The boisterous game put an end to Kariyakutty's concentration. Words were exchanged, which then turned into a brawl with fisticuffs and rolling on the ground, and in the middle of it, Paulochan clamped his teeth around Kariyakutty's ear. Try as he might, Kariyakutty could not free himself, and by the time Mariyamma and Kuncheriya came running and made Paulochan let go, a piece of the ear was in his mouth. Matters did not end there. When Paulochan spat out the piece of flesh, their two-year-old brother Babu, who was standing by watching the fight, picked it up and put it in his mouth. Mariyamma, leaving the crying and bleeding Kariyakutty temporarily, tried to take it out of the child's mouth, but he had, by then, swallowed it.

Overcome with pain, sadness and, above all else, shame, Kariyakutty looked at Yonankunju and Paulochan. 'Spawn of serpents, you all will rot for this!' he declared.

Occupied as she was with taking Kariyakutty to the doctor, Mariyamma could not punish Yonankunju and Paulochan. All she could do, as she left, was to fix them with a look and say, 'Just you wait until your appachan gets home…'

The boys ignored her threat, knowing fully well at what time and in what condition their appachan would come home. But, unfortunately for them, even though Geevarghese got home way past midnight, he was not entirely the worse for wear, and the night ended with the boys receiving a feast of thrashing.

Of the thirteen children born to Geevarghese and Mariyamma, Yonankunju and Paulochan were the unruliest, and it was they who received the most thrashing from Geevarghese. Consequently, they had an abiding anger towards their father, an anger with an intensity only children can muster. One time, after being punished for something or the other, they decided to exact revenge. They dug a hole in Geevarghese's regular path home and disguised its opening with dry leaves and twigs. No one else took that path in the middle of the night, and they hoped that their father would step into it, breaking, at the very least, his ankle. Unfortunately for them, it was a stray piebald dog that fell into the hole. He climbed out of it and walked away with a slight limp, leaving the hole gaping for anyone to see. It is not clear whether the dog had actually broken his leg or whether it was broken only psychosomatically. Or whether he had simply decided to limp as he went on his way because he had fallen into a hole, and falling into a hole usually involved the breaking of a limb.

Until Yonankunju was thirteen and Paulochan was twelve, they were inseparable, sharing their food, their bed and their mischiefs. But things changed abruptly. One day, it was discovered that some money had gone missing from the house – just a few paise, to be clear. All thefts in Kottarathil Veedu could usually be traced back to Yonankunju and Paulochan, and so Geevarghese caught hold of Paulochan, pulled out a kaashav plant and began thrashing him with it. This plant, kaashav, has a peculiarity. It has a hard main stem which produces eight or ten side shoots which are almost as hard. So, when one is thrashed with it, which is usually only done in instances of grave crimes, it is equivalent to being thrashed with ten switches at the same time. Two or three plants tied together would make a good broom. The plant is usually used for these two main purposes – discipline and cleanliness.

No matter how severe the punishment, Yonankunju and Paulochan had, until that day, never told on one another. But, for whatever reason, on that day, as soon as the third whack fell, Paulochan wailed, 'It wasn't meeeee! It was Yonankunjuuuuu!' and promptly fell to the ground in a faint. Geevarghese left him there and went after Yonankunju and thrashed the living daylights out of him. All through it, Yonankunju stood firm as a rock, the betrayal of his brother burning up inside him. It was Geevarghese who finally gave up, panting with the exertion of punishing his son. After the thrashing was done, Paulochan went up to his brother.

'Do not talk to me ever again,' Yonankunju said before Paulochan could say anything. 'You and I – we're done.'

From that day on, whenever they ran into each other, they would pretend to be strangers. They did not even attend each other's weddings. Forty years would pass before they would speak again, and that too, over the phone. 'My daughter is getting married on the fourteenth of next month. You must come,' Yonankunju would tell Paulochan. 'Of course, I'll be there,' Paulochan would reply. And that would end the enmity.

Since Kariyakutty lived apart from everyone else, Mariyamma often forgot about her eldest son. Once when an official from a government department came to do some survey and asked about her children, Mariyamma told him, correctly, that she had thirteen. But no matter how many times she recited their names, counting them out on her fingers and toes, she could only come up with twelve. Overcome with embarrassment and feeling the pressure to give a proper account to the government official, she tried to arrive at the right number by including Susanna's name twice. But the official saw right through her trick. Finally, it was Marykochu, who was standing by watching her mother, who said, 'Ammachi, you forgot Kariyakutty kunjanja.'

'Oh, my Lord, how could I forget the name of my own child,' cried Mariyamma, and continued weeping for the next two or three hours.

His family and his neighbours were convinced that Kariyakutty would grow up to become a vishuddhan, a saint. But in his twelfth year on this earth, entirely unexpectedly, Kariyakutty returned to the abode of God. An ordinary fever, that was all it was to begin with, which only required Neelandan Vaidyan's medicine and a couple of days' rest. In the evening of the second day, he expressed a desire to eat some pidi and meat curry. Mariyamma, aware that it was the first time her son had made such a request, quickly wrung the neck of a hen and made the curry and the little rice dumplings. Kariyakutty ate it, exclaiming in between mouthfuls, 'Ooh, so tasty!' He ate until his stomach was about to burst. Then, he belched loudly and began to cry.

'Oh, my Lord … such tasty things were in this world, and I lived all this while slurping up kanjivellam,' he wailed. 'Sod it all, it's too late now … my time is up!'

And within half an hour, Kariyakutty, who should have been a saint, left his worldly life.

The person who was most affected by Kariyakutty's death was Anna valyamma. For a long time now, the sole defining purpose of her life was to bear witness to Kariyakutty's miraculous deeds. She was entering the dusk of her life, and was beginning to feel remorseful about the things she had done in pursuit of bodily pleasure. She had hoped that Kariyakutty, once he attained sainthood, would intervene with Karthav Eesho Mishiha on her behalf at the time of the reckoning of her sins and get Him to release her from the dreadful punishment that awaited her, or at the very least, get it reduced. When she thought about the type of sin her grandson would have to haggle over with the Lord, she was overcome with shame and unease. Still, the important thing – the only important thing, really – was to escape from the unextinguishable fire and the indestructible worms of damnation in hell. With Kariyakutty's death, Anna valyamma was certain that she was headed straight for hell. This thought and the flames of remorse and fear that burned her alive had almost driven her to madness over the years when, thankfully, she was captured by dementia. Anna valyamma spent the rest of her years as happy and innocent as a child. And just like a child, she fought tooth and nail when she was forced to share the things she loved – snacks, the swing, a toy bus made of wood, a red-and-white ball, a madamma doll dressed in a blue frock, a green plastic parrot – with someone else. This 'someone else' usually, of course, was Maria, and she was the rightful owner of all the things mentioned in the list, except for the snacks. And yet, Maria got to play with them only when Anna valyamma was otherwise occupied or out of sight. But these were things yet to happen.

After Kariyakutty's death, the relationship between Anna valyamma and Kariyakutty transformed into something different. When she misplaced things, Anna valyamma would call on him. 'Eda, Kariyakutty, where are Valyammachi's reading glasses, son? Reveal them to me.'

Of Kariyakutty's surviving siblings, all except Neena and Thomachan grew up without trouble and went on to find good jobs and make good lives. Other than reading the Congress-friendly reports in the newspapers, Thomachan did not let any of the world's problems affect him or have an impact on his personal life. He gave up his studies early on and sat at home doing nothing, and he continued doing nothing for an entire lifetime.

Neena's life, meanwhile, took a different direction. Happy in her own company from a very young age, she liked to be alone.

Kottarathil Veedu had several rooms and corridors, but it was Neena who actualized the idea of 'a room of one's own' for the first time in its confines. She made sure that she stayed out of sight of the others, and since there were so many members in the family, no one really bothered to find out what she got up to by herself behind closed doors. Neena passed the Class 10 exams with good marks, but decided to discontinue her studies and dedicated herself to sitting in a room with its doors closed for the entire day. When she was of marriageable age and proposals began to arrive, Geevarghese and Kuncheriya picked one that seemed suitable – Elias from Mundakkayam, a planter. They asked Neena for her opinion, but she had no opinion on her own marriage.

The marriage caused an earthquake in Planter Elias's home and hometown. Right from the day after the wedding, the new bride began sitting in a room with its doors shut. The mother-in-law, Kunjoonjamma, who had been waiting to pass on, with all its intensity, the torture she had suffered from her own mother-in-law, stood confounded faced with this situation. And Elias's sister, Salomi, who had abandoned her husband and two children to their devices and come home with the singular objective of exercising her right as the sister-in-law to torment the new bride, also did not know what to do. How could they torture a person if that person was nowhere to be seen! When they did run into each other, Kunjoonjamma tried to begin an attack, but Neena pretended not to hear or see anything. Salomi was not ready to accept defeat that easily. In the week after the wedding, she dismissed Mathu and Tharamma, two of the servants whose sole job was to wash the dirty dishes in the kitchen, and commanded Neena to take over. With the labourers working in the plantation and the considerable number of family members to feed, washing dirty dishes was a day-long job that required two sets of hands at least. Neena did the washing quietly and without complaint.

When the last of the dishes was washed, Neena turned to Salomi. 'Nathooney,' she said, addressing Salomi properly as sister-in-law, 'there's no point in you freeloading over here, abandoning your husband and children. If you or your mother think you can work me like a donkey, think again. I washed that mountain of dishes just now only to prove to you that I know how to do it. But from tomorrow, not one person in this house will eat in a plate Neena has cleaned. So, go, get lost!' And she went back to her room and shut the door.

The person who suffered the most was Elias. He would never recover from the embarrassing situation he found himself in on his wedding night, witnessed by his family members and relatives and neighbours, of having to knock, for over fifteen minutes, on the door to his bridal suite to get his wife to let him in. In actual fact, Neena had not intended for that to happen; it was just force of habit. But she did not bother explaining this to Elias. Kunjoonjamma hassled her son constantly to put an end to his wife's disdainful isolation of herself in her room. But every attempt Elias made to question Neena about this, she silenced with a piercing look. In any case, by this time, husbands who kept their wives subjugated under their fists were fast becoming an endangered species.

Despite the closed door that stood between them like the Great Wall of China, Elias produced two children with Neena. After the second confinement, when Elias tried to sidle up to her, Neena declared: 'Listen to me, don't expect me to reproduce year in, year out like my ammachi. I've made two for you. Now let me be.'

With that, she began sleeping in a separate bedroom. Not to be outdone, and quietly hoping that Neena would come to her senses, Elias began to spend his nights with the servant woman, Molamma. But Neena's only response was to behave more affectionately towards Molamma. It was Neena who protested when an irate Kunjoonjamma tried to banish Molamma from the house. When, in the ensuing tussle, Molamma was seriously hurt, it was Neena who looked after her. And when Elias caught chickenpox and lay helpless in Molamma's bed, Neena went into the tiny little room and nursed him back to health.

But the incidents that followed stunned even those who knew Neena well, including Geevarghese. One day, when a woman, very old and barely able to walk, came begging for alms, Neena invited her in and bade her stay with them. She cooked three meals a day — sometimes even four, the old woman had an insatiable appetite — and fed her with her own hands. Kunjoonjamma had gone to visit Salomi, so it was a while before she heard of the development. And when she returned, what welcomed her was the sight of the strange old woman sitting on a chair with one leg crossed over the other, watching *Chitrahaar*. Rajesh Khanna was chucking a flower at a whimpering Asha Parekh in an effort to placate her, and the old woman was whimpering right alongside while also snacking on a plate of freshly fried pazhampori. She was not pleased when someone walked in, interrupting her. At that precise moment, there was a break in transmission, and the inscription apologizing for it — 'Rukavat ke liye khed hai' — along with the image of a wire fence and a Petromax lamp came up on the television screen.

'Who are you?' asked the old woman in an angry voice.

Kunjoonjamma faltered at this unexpected questioning in her own home. Luckily for her, Molamma came out and took her inside and explained what had been going on. Shaking with rage, Kunjoonjamma went into the kitchen where Neena was busy chopping meat to make a curry for the old woman.

'Endhyanichi! You won't rest until you have bankrupted us, will you? Hussy!' she screeched, rushing towards Neena.

Neena looked up, her face devoid of expression, and pointed the knife at her. 'I'll gut you,' she said calmly, and turned away, back to her chore.

Quietly exclaiming, 'Oh, it's so hot these days,' Kunjoonjamma left the kitchen and went into her room. She was rarely seen outside the house after that incident. Within a couple of years, and perhaps because she was so distressed, she decided to return to the abode of God.

Over the years, Neena invited home anyone and everything that went down the road – beggars, vagabonds, mad people, dogs, cats, pangolins ... Meanwhile, Elias ... well, it is probably best not to talk about what went on with him.

By the time these incidents happened, Geevarghese had given up his public life and withdrawn into the confines of Kottarathil Veedu. He did wonder whether it was his fault that Neena had turned out this way, whether there was something wrong in the way he had brought her up. 'Ah, what could I have done? People turn out the way they are, depending on what is written on their head. Besides, look at Paulochan, Babu, Anna, Susanna and the rest. I brought them up too, didn't I, and they turned out all right.' If Geevarghese's children could have heard his thoughts, they would have died laughing. 'Brought up? Who brought up whom?' Whatever 'bringing up' there was, it was done by Kuncheriya and by poor, beleaguered Mariyamma.

It was Susanna, the oldest of the children, who inherited Mariyamma's culinary prowess and her motherly nature, while

Anna got her beauty. And it was this Anna who would become Maria's mother. But nothing can be said about Anna in Maria's story because Maria and Anna barely knew each other. And as the Geevarghese who Anna knew and the Geevarghese who Maria knew were two entirely different people, it is best if we let him tell his own story.

# 7

# Geevarghese's Story

I was named in honour of our punyalachan, the patron saint of our land, Geevarghese Sahada. According to custom, my name should have been Mathu, the name of my grandfather, my appan's appan. But the day before I was born, my ammachi ate a shitload of boiled tapioca, and so, when it was time to push me out, she was in trouble. My valyammachi, Mathiri, made a deal with the punyalachan that if I came out all right, she would name me after him. That is how I, who should have been Mathu, became Geevarghese.

Anyhow, I came out of the womb more or less unharmed. When he heard about the underhand deal his wife had made with Geevarghese Sahada, my valyappachan exploded with anger – and it was the only time he was ever seen to be angry at Valyammachi – but he controlled himself given that the party that wronged him, more than Valyammachi herself, was, after all, the punyalachan.

My ammachi always said that I was a very pretty child. But let's take that with a pinch of salt because she was besotted with me. I, on the other hand, hated her. She stank of onions.

Unlike Maria, I don't remember much about my childhood. Maria says that her ability to remember things has decreased after she was given back to her parents. I am not sure if that is true. After all, she was only six or seven when she was given back, and loss of memory at that age is unheard of among human beings. But this is Maria we are talking about, so who knows! She once told me about something that had happened when she was not even a year old. My ammachi was on her deathbed. I was standing next to her with the ten-month-old Maria on my hip. Thinking that it was time for her to go, Ammachi asked to be turned towards the west. Mariyamma leaned in to help me turn her. Suddenly, Ammachi screeched: 'I've already taken my last sacrament. Don't you touch me and make me dirty!' Poor Mariyamma. Mortified, she was. Ammachi lay facing west for a whole day before getting up from her deathbed and walking into the kitchen saying she had a hankering to eat ripe jackfruit.

I have lived here, in this land where I was born, all my life. Maria says I should have been born in Brazil. Still, I have lived quite happily here. Nowadays, you can't call this place a village. Kerala has no more villages, they said that on the TV the other day. In my childhood, it was towns we didn't have. Then again, my childhood was over eighty years ago, wasn't it?

My first memory is of my appan throwing a pot at my ammachi. Over the years, Appan has thrown several things at Ammachi, but she has, with excellent dexterity, avoided being hit by any of them. It could also be that Appan missed on purpose, worried that physical abuse of his wife might affect his eventual ascent to heaven. Everyone considered my appan to be a saintly person. It was as though he was born with the sole purpose of going to heaven. I could never understand why he was so tempted by heaven, this place no one has ever seen.

When I think of my childhood, the first person I remember is Mathiri valyammachi. A phenomenon, she was! Prophesying was her favourite pastime. Let me tell you something I have seen with my own two eyes. I must have been eight or nine at the time. One day, our parish priest, Vettikkattil Kathanar, came home and began admonishing Mathiri valyammachi saying that prophesying was not something good Christians got up to. Valyammachi sat there nodding along obediently until Kathanar, with a great sense of self-importance and satisfaction, worked himself to the end of his speech.

The moment he finished speaking, Valyammachi pointed to the ceiling. 'Look, Father,' she said, 'that rafter will fall on your head right now.'

And, lo and behold, before she could even finish her sentence, the rafter fell on Kathanar's head and he began bleeding. To this day, I have no idea how that sturdy piece of wood broke off just like that. Anyway, the moment it fell, I started laughing, and the priest cursed me and said that I was headed straight to hell. Like I said, I was only about eight or nine, so what did I care about heaven and hell!

My grandfather, Kottarathil Mathu, was the second person to approach Valyammachi's family with a marriage proposal. Her family had already fixed her marriage to the first person, but Valyammachi kept insisting that it was Mathu from Kottarathil Veedu who would be her husband. Her family had never even heard of this Kottarathil Veedu or of Mathu. Up to that point, Valyammachi's prophesying was at the level of predicting when a jackfruit would fall off the tree or when the hen would lay an egg, so no one took her seriously. A week later, a messenger came from the prospective groom's house with the news that he had passed away. He had sat down to have his morning kanji and felt somewhat unwell, and next thing you knew, he was dead! Valyammachi's family was in a great quandary. The first proposal had come to nothing, but neither Mathu nor Kottarathil Veedu had made an appearance on the scene yet.

What followed was truly the handiwork of God. Without His interference none of it would have happened. Mathu had a herd bull that was famous across the land, and one fine day, it went missing. Since three heifers ready to be mated – fair-skinned Velumbi, broken-horned Kombi, and another nameless one – were in the cattle shed, the bull was tethered to the tamarind tree in the yard and was being pampered. When Chakki came out with a bucket of coconut pumice for the bull, he was nowhere to be seen. She ran around looking for it, and eventually called in Kunjikkali, Paramu and Chathan who were working in the compound to help. They searched all over the place but could not find even the shadow of the bull. Puzzled, people scratched their noses, wondering how such an enormous bull could disappear just like that.

No amount of scratched noses would bring the bull back, though, would it? There were other herd bulls in the neighbourhood, but none of them met Mathu's exacting standards. So, he set out in search of a new herd bull. Now, as we all know, it is common for countryfolk to set out to the house next door for something and find themselves fifty miles away. It was even more so in the olden days.

Mathu heard about a herd bull that was available for sale at Manamel Veedu, a house two or three miles away. But when he got there, he realized the journey had been for nothing.

'Aiyo! We sold it last week only,' said the bull's owner, Outha. 'You should have come a week earlier.'

How could Mathu have gone looking for it a week earlier? He had his own herd bull then. Anyway, when Outha told him about a bull belonging to a man named Koruthu, they decided to go to his house. But when they got there, Koruthu had no bull to sell to them. The search continued, but there were no bulls to be found.

Finally, after walking around for two days, Mathu got to the house of Kunjippalu, almost thirty miles away from Kottarathil Veedu. Kunjippalu's wife Naithy opened the door. The moment she heard the name 'Kottarathil Mathu', she called out to Karthav Eesho Mishiha and fell down in a dead faint. Years would pass, and Mathu would always wonder why his mother-in-law fainted when she saw him for the first time.

My great-grandmother Naithy had only one piece of advice for her daughter before her wedding: stop prophesying. But Valyammachi ignored the advice and continued her prophecies. She was fifteen when she got married. My valyappachan was very fond of my valyammachi. When he expressed a desire to be the father of a son, Valyammachi told him that it would be another ten years before they had a child. And exactly ten years later, when no one retained even the remote hope that Mathiri valyammachi would become a mother, she proclaimed she was pregnant with a boy.

My appan, Kuncheriya, was the product of that pregnancy. Despite having been born after ten long years of waiting, Valyappachan and Appan were never close. Besides, friendships between parents and children were not in fashion in those days.

Anyhow, two years later, they had another son – my kochappan Paulo, Mathachan's father. Mathachan spent most of his younger years in our house. Valyappachan had a much closer, almost warm, relationship with Paulo kochappan, the son who had inherited his love for the soil and for farming. While my appan spent his time immersed in other-worldly matters, Paulo kochappan and Valyappachan tilled the soil, sowed the seeds, and harvested the crops. No small task looking after land that stretched all the way to the horizon. It was difficult to work this land and get back home every day, so Paulo kochappan built a temporary house at the other end of the property. After his marriage, he rebuilt it into a proper, impressive house and moved permanently into it. This is how, contrary to the custom that the youngest son inherited the ancestral house, my appan came to be the owner of Kottarathil Veedu.

Valyappachan, in his fondness for Mathiri valyammachi, would buy her lots of fabric to make her chatta and mundu. Valyammachi would have a couple of sets made and use the rest of the fabric to make animals. She was not very good at it though, so the monkeys, elephants and cats she made did not resemble the animals in any way, shape or form. She made a new toy once and gave it to me saying it was a monkey. 'It doesn't look anything like a monkey,' I said, and she said, 'Well, this is how a monkey should look, it's just that God made a mistake!'

Anna valyamma was scared of Mathiri valyammachi. Despite the fact that it was Valyammachi who gave Anna valyamma asylum in Kottarathil Veedu, she tried to make herself inconspicuous around Valyammachi. Until she came to Kottarathil Veedu at the age of thirteen, Anna valyamma had suffered from starvation. The day she arrived, having eaten her fill for the first time in her entire life, Anna valyamma had gas trouble and chest pain. Her gas-filled stomach hardened like a stone, and for three days she suffered, unable to stand or sit. And for all those three days, she squatted behind whatever cover she could find, trying to take a shit. Remember, there were no toilets in those days, so you could sit anywhere out in the open as you pleased. Finally, on the third night, it came out, everything she had eaten three days ago, in exactly the same form. Her stomach was not used to so much food, so it didn't know how to digest it. Over the next three days, Anna valyamma pushed out everything she had ever eaten since the day she was born. Wherever one looked, there would be Anna valyamma, straining in a squatting position. After those six days of toil, for the next three days, the only food Mathiri valyammachi allowed Anna valyamma to have was the bitter juice of kaipakka. On the second day, Anna valyamma baulked, refusing to drink it. 'Do you want to shit again?' asked Mathiri valyammachi, her voice all grave. She had barely finished her question before Anna valyamma ran outside, overcome by the urge to squat. After that, she drank the juice without complaint, without one word of protest. When Valyammachi left the room, Anna valyamma turned to Kunjeetha, Eetha's mother who used to look after the kitchen in those days. 'Odekkaara!' she said. 'What a woman!' Anyway, after that Anna valyamma did not suffer from any type of stomach complaints, except that, whenever she ran into Mathiri valyammachi, a quiver would run through her stomach.

I think that, just like my name, Mathiri valyammachi knew all about my life and my destiny way before I was even born. I am not sure I believe the tapioca–Geevarghese Sahada origin story entirely because Valyammachi had no real involvement with the church or its matters. There is a story that, in order to avoid going to church, she had spread out her 'four unclean days' across the four Sundays in a month. Remember, it was a time when the church was way too interested in the cleanliness and purity of women. It seems Vettikkattil Kathanar said, on hearing about Valyammachi's monthlies that came over four Sundays, that it was Karthaveeshomishiha punishing her, preventing her from ever entering the church. I can't stop laughing even now when I think about it … As if Our Lord Jesus Christ has nothing else to do!

Like I said, Valyammachi knew everything before it happened. Once, my ammachi was sitting in the kitchen veranda, eating papaya.

'Pregnant women should not eat papaya,' Valyammachi told her. 'It's bad for the little boy inside.'

Ammachi, who was certain that there was no one – boy or girl – inside her womb, ignored her and continued eating her papaya. Two or three weeks passed, and Ammachi's monthlies stopped. Appan, who knew all about Valyammachi's prophecies, was overjoyed about the imminent arrival of his son and began to make plans. He even said that he would make his son – me – a bishop. Valyammachi listened to his plans and said, 'Kuncheriya, it's best that you don't put too much stock in him.' One time, Ammachi expressed her doubt whether I, as a person, was endowed with feelings such as love and kindness. 'That papaya you ate when you were pregnant, that's the reason,' Valyammachi told her. 'It sucked out all tender feelings from the child in the womb.' Have you ever heard such crazy talk!

There was this cow, Velumbi, that wouldn't become pregnant even after several mating sessions. Valyappachan decided to sell her to the butchers, and when they came to collect the cow, Valyammachi sent them back saying it was not for sale. Then she looked at Valyappachan. 'It's not Velumbi's destiny to die sterile,' she said, all serious like. Poor Valyappachan … didn't know where to look. Barely a year went by, and there was Velumbi – pregnant! From then on, for many years to come, Velumbi would give birth twice every year. She seemed to have suddenly developed a fertility that was unheard of in any animal before or since.

I began drinking toddy at a very young age. It was a habit that started quite unexpectedly. Chathan, who tapped the palms in our compounds, liked to have a little slurp of the toddy as soon as the pots were brought down from the trees. If there was a small plate of fish curry to accompany the toddy, so much the better. So, I began stealing fish curry for Chathan from the kitchen, and to express his gratitude, he began to give me a little toddy poured into a tin mug. I didn't steal the fish curry to get toddy in return, that is the honest truth. I did it just for the thrill of stealing from one's own home – a thrill that cannot be described and can only be understood fully through experience.

One day, as I walked into the kitchen, I ran into Valyammachi. 'This is just the beginning of things to come,' she told me. 'You'll spend your entire life stealing. From your own home.' She did not tell me that I should stop this habit, but I did. If someone knows we are stealing, then it is not really stealing, is it? It killed the thrill.

The other day, Maria asked me whether life was more fun then or now. 'Then, obviously,' I told her. In those days, one rarely needed to pay for the toddy one drank. It was like water. Does anyone pay for water? Well, yes, one can buy water in shops these days, but if my ancestors were to hear of such a thing, they would not believe it. How can water be sold, they would ask. I heard on TV the other day that some government was selling off a river. What! Have the people in that land lost their tongues? In my youth, if someone came around saying that the river belonged to them, they wouldn't go back walking. These days, though, sell off a river and no one will say a word. Times sure have changed!

What Valyammachi said about the papaya sucking out all my tender feelings ... it is not entirely true. There has to be some goodness in you if you are a human being, and I have always had great love for such people – Mathiri valyammachi, Mathu valyappachan, Kelan, Velayudhan, Kali, Maria ... As for Appan, Ammachi, Mariyamma and my children ... what is there to love? I can't love somebody just because we are related.

Let me tell you about the time when Valyammachi got a parrot ... Oh, she was a wayward and contrary creature. We named her Ammini and taught her to talk. The first thing Valyammachi taught her was 'Shoshamma-mandi' – stupid-Shoshamma. As you know, Shoshamma was my ammachi's name. I was only nine years old at the time. Still, I told Valyammachi to stop behaving like a child. Parrots are like children, she told me, they only understand such simple things. Ammini – like children? Ha! That creature was devious!

Ammini had very specific likes and dislikes. She could not stand the sight of Shoshamma-mandi. Knowing Ammini, one would think that she would not like Anna valyamma either, but she really took to her. It was Valyammachi who found out the reason. 'The person Ammini dislikes the most is Shoshamma, and Anna too can't stand Shoshamma. It is because they have this dislike in common that Ammini likes Anna.' I said I didn't agree with this reasoning because, as far as I could see, Anna valyamma worshipped Ammachi. Valyammachi did not say anything immediately, but that night, she took me to Anna valyamma's bedroom. And there she was, Anna valyamma, cursing my ammachi loudly in her sleep! I have checked this out many times after that, and every night I went into her room, I heard her cursing away to glory. So, I finally understood the actual status of the relationship between Ammachi and Anna valyamma.

If there was one thing that confused Ammini, it was names. For example, she heard different people calling Valyammachi by different names. My appan and Ammachi called her 'Ammachi' because she was their mother. I called her 'Valyammachi' because she was my grandmother. My valyappachan called her 'Mathiri' because, as her husband, he called her by her given name. Anna valyamma called her 'Valyamma' because she considered her to be an aunt. The servants called her 'Kochamma' because she was their mistress. Everyone in the household had such multiple names which caused Ammini no end of confusion. But clever clogs that she was, she found a solution to the problem herself. She began calling everyone by what their elders called them. So, I was Geevarghese, Valyammachi was Mathiri, Appan was Kuncheriya, and Anna valyamma was Anna. All except Ammachi, who remained Shoshamma-mandi. Still, one confusion remained. There was no one older than Valyappachan in the household. Valyammachi called him 'Athey-nney' – something to mean 'look here' or 'listen'. So, Ammini decided that was his name and began to call him Athey-nney.

Ammini assumed that Mathachan, Paulo kochappan's son, who visited often was my appan's son. The moment she saw him, she would call out, 'Kuncheriya, your son is here...' And immediately, from somewhere near the kitchen, would come Ammachi's screech, 'This confounded parrot!'

Valyammachi was my grandmother as well as his, and yet Mathachan always referred to her as 'your valyammachi'. 'When you get to hell, they will slash you and your valyammachi all over, marinate you in salt, chilli powder and a bit of black pepper, and fry you in hot oil,' he told me one time. He had meant to scare me, but I laughed imagining us all nice and crispy. I told Valyammachi this and she went, 'Don't you know? Fried meat is his favourite food.' Mathachan was a bit of a mischief-maker until about twelve years old, but after that he changed. Started sitting somewhere quietly, lost in some daydream. A romantic type, like Maria says.

Then there was that time when Valyammachi and Ammini fell out with one another. It was only a small spat to begin with, but it grew into an almighty quarrel. Ammini accused Valyammachi of being ungrateful, while Valyammachi said she did not know what she was supposed to be grateful for. I am the best companion Mathiri could ever hope for, claimed Ammini. She's just exaggerating her role, countered Valyammachi. The whole thing got out of hand, and Ammini began to act out and started calling Valyammachi 'Mathiri-mandi'. To retaliate, Valyammachi got a crow from somewhere and set it up in a cage next to Ammini's and proceeded to teach it to talk. Looking crossly at Ammini and Valyammachi, the crow began to recite its lessons:

Geevarghese

Kraa kraa kraa

Mathiri

Kraa kraa

Kuncheriya

Kraa kraa kraa

Anna

Kraaaaa

Listening to the class, Ammini and I died laughing. Ammini would pause every now and then, and say somewhat philosophically, 'Everyone has a destiny. There's nothing anyone can do to change it.'

Finally, heeding my relentless pleas, Valyammachi let the crow out of the cage. Just before it went on its way, the crow flew straight at Ammini with the express purpose of murdering her. Valyammachi jumped in and saved her from certain death, and with that, a compromise was reached.

Like I said, Ammini was very clever, but there were times when she acted like she had no common sense. Once, when the priest Vettikkattil Kathanar came home, Ammini began singing, ever so sweetly: *Karthave njaan bharthavillathezhu pettu* ... You know the song – the one about the woman without a husband who gave birth to seven children, who all died thanks to Our Lord Karthav's mercy.

The horrified Kathanar sprang up from his seat. 'Who has taught this creature this vile song?' he screamed.

The question, obviously, was not addressed to Ammini, but she chose to answer anyway.

'Mathiri,' she said coolly.

When Valyammachi died, Ammini stopped speaking. Many years would pass before she would speak again. And then one day, out of the blue, she said, 'Listen, I didn't speak because I didn't want to, not because I couldn't.' From then on, she would say this every now and then, and until her death, those were the only words she ever spoke.

Much later, I bought Maria a parrot. The bird was not as clever as Ammini but could speak quite fluently. Well, one fine day, Chandippatti upped and killed it! 'Why would you do such a beastly thing,' I asked him, and you know what he said? He said I shouldn't have brought such a stupid creature home. 'But didn't you hear how well it spoke,' I asked him. 'What is important is not how well one speaks but what one says,' he declared.

I was the one who taught Valyammachi, over a period of time, to read and write. Ammachi did not like it one bit. 'Already the old hag is crazy,' she muttered several times a day, 'and now that she is literate, who knows what all will happen.' The day she was able to write the word 'Mathiri', Valyammachi made payasam all by herself. Well, I say payasam, but it was more like ... let's just say that Valyammachi was never too keen on cooking. Then one day, she declared that she didn't like the name Mathiri and that henceforth her name would be Ursula. I don't know where she came up with that wacky name. Is that even a name? In any case, no one really cared except poor Valyappachan. Every now and then, Valyammachi would put her foot down and succeed in making him call her Ursula, and each time he uttered the name, Valyappachan would be mortified and turn red. But the person who was most affected by this change of name was Ammini. She became utterly confused and began calling Valyammachi 'Uthiri' and 'Moorsula'. If you ask me, she did it on purpose, devious little thing that she was. Thankfully, though, Valyammachi lost interest in the name quite quickly. She was like that, you know, never could keep her interest in anything for too long. Maria is just like her.

Once she learned the letters, Valyammachi began writing all over the walls of the house with pieces of coal. I asked her what she was writing. 'I am rewriting the Bible,' she replied, but she didn't look as though she was engaged in such a responsible task. She clambered up a ladder and began at the top of the walls. When she had scribbled all over the walls of two rooms, Appan got involved. By then, Valyappachan had been dead for years. Appan summoned Eenashu, the man who looked after our household, sent him up on a ladder and ordered him to wash the rewritten Bible off the walls. As Eenashu picked up a broom and began climbing up the ladder, Valyammachi declared: 'Eenashu, if you step on that ladder, you won't come down with your feet on the ground.' Eenashu ignored her and climbed up. But just as he was about to splash water all over the new scripture on the wall, there he was! Sprawled on the floor! It took three months of daily massages to return his injured back to normal while the new Bible escaped with not even one of its letters erased. And Appan, who anyway was scared of Valyammachi's prophecies, never again attempted to cause it harm. For years to come, that Bible was a miracle in our land. I still remember our countryfolk bringing their visiting relatives to see the Bible and how they stood before it dumbstruck. After Valyammachi's death, Appan waited only a few days before demolishing the walls, new Bible and all, and building an altogether new house in its place. I regret, deeply, that I was in no position to preserve that revised version of the Bible for the edification of generations to come.

Valyammachi was excellent at making up odd, confounding stories, mixing up tales from the Bible, the Ramayanam, the Mahabharatham and folklore. I was her one and only audience. Here's one story:

> Once upon a time, there was a king named Kumbhakarnan. He was as big as an elephant and slept all the time. All he did was eat and sleep. The moment he woke up, he would shout, 'Who's there? Bring us something to eat!' One time, the king was travelling in a boat, and of course, he promptly fell asleep. The boat began to keel over because of the king's weight, and the boatmen, scared for their own lives, picked up the king and threw him in the water. A blue whale spotted the king floating in the water. 'Oh, an elephant! If I eat this elephant, I won't have to eat anything for at least another year,' it thought, and swallowed the king. For the whale, anything that big had to be an elephant. After all, it didn't know about kings and all, did it?
> 
> But the moment it swallowed its meal, the whale realized it had swallowed more than it could stomach. Its tummy began to ache. And what an ache it was too! Every time the king twisted and turned in its tummy, the whale suffered indescribable pain.

And then one day, the king woke up and roared: 'Who's there? Bring us our food!' The pain was one thing, and now this racket from its own tummy ... The whale was truly confounded. Meanwhile, since no one brought him anything to eat, the hungry king began to take bites of the whale's stomach wall.

Unable to stand the pain any longer, the whale began to beat its head against a rock. 'Whatever is the matter?' asked the rock, because the rock was really a turtle. When the weeping whale told the turtle everything, the turtle took it to a doctor in its acquaintance. And the doctor, assisted ably by two hundred junior doctors, cut its tummy open, and out came a man in tears! It was not the king, but a prophet. He told them that his name was Jonah, that he had become King Kumbhakarnan because of a curse, and that he had finally been released from the curse as a result of being swallowed by a fish. The whale heard the mention of its part in the tale. 'I am not a fish,' it said from the operation table where they were stitching up its tummy. 'I am a whale, a blue whale.' Jonah, meanwhile, could not decide whether he was supposed to go back to his life as Jonah or as Kumbhakarnan. In the end, he decided to spend the rest of his life with the doctor as his helper.

And here is another of Valyammachi's stories...

One time, Ravanan's sister, Soorpanakha, went all the way to Israel to marry Abraham's son, Isahaq. You must have heard of such princesses, the type who fall in love the moment they hear a story about someone ... Soorpanakha was such a princess. When she was little, she had heard stories of Abraham's sacrifice. What she felt at first towards Isahaq was pity and empathy – 'Oh, the poor dear!' – but gradually it turned into love, and that's when she decided to go to Israel and become his wife. But by the time she got there, after years and years of journeying by sea, Soorpanakha had become an old woman, and Isahaq had already married Rebecca.

Valyammachi was like that – ending stories abruptly, abrasively! 'The Ramayanam and the Mahabharatham were written by people who had creative sensibilities, but the Bible lacks such artistic flair,' she would declare. Perhaps that was the reason she decided to rewrite the Bible.

Towards the end of her days, Valyammachi began to complain about a rank smell, like something was decaying. And then suddenly one day she declared: 'Odekkaara! It is me who's stinking of decay!' That year during the church festival, she bought some dark blue cloth at the festival market and got a chatta and mundu made up. 'Dress me in these when I'm dead,' she told everyone, and explained her reason. 'When I get to heaven, I want Karthaveeshomishiha to recognize me immediately.'

When they brought her to her funeral dressed in those dark blue clothes, Vettikkattil Kathanar refused to bury her at first. But the repercussions of going against Valyammachi's wishes were evidenced in the two-inch scar still visible on his forehead. And when Appan pressed a large wad of cash into his hands, Valyammachi was interred in our family grave without further ado. Even now, Mathiri valyammachi is famous in these parts as the first person ever to go to her burial in coloured clothes.

By the time I was fifteen, I began to avoid my home as much as possible. I didn't like my appan who was always bothering God, but I disliked even more my ammachi who followed me with her annoying and excessive love. It was only much later in life, when I watched Mariyamma bringing up our children, that I understood that this problem was not confined to my ammachi. All women were born like this. They were unaware of a world that existed beyond their husband and children. They were uninterested in finding out if such a world existed, nor were they interested in letting others find out. If they could tie up their husband and children inside the house, they would be overjoyed. It is my opinion that mothers and wives are responsible for making the husbands of the world selfish and shiftless.

My first companion in the world outside my home was Kelan. Then came Velayudhan, Paramu ... Still, it is Kali who comes into my memory first, but I can't say anything about her. It was only after she ran away with the hawker Thimman that I realized what a big part she had in my life. That time we went to see the sea, as we stood watching it together, the desire to spend the rest of my days with her had filled my heart. But, what to do, soon after we came back from watching the sea, she ran away! If she had hung around longer, I would surely have left Mariyamma and would be living with Kali now.

Everyone thinks that I became friends with people from the lower castes just to rebel. This is not true. In those days, upper castes didn't frequent toddy shops or want to be friends with someone like me who had a bad reputation. So, I became friends with people from the lower castes, and very soon began to feel genuine love for them. We didn't know what was happening in the world, and none of us, except Kelan, had any interest in finding out.

One time ... I must have been around twenty years of age then. Velayudhan came to the toddy shop with a section of the newspaper he had found on the road. In it was the picture of an aeroplane and a story about flying. It was the first time any of us had set eyes on such a thing. We were under the impression, until then, that the only things that flew were birds, angels and ghosts.

Velayudhan: What do they take us for? Fools? To make us believe that this thing can fly?

Kelan: What about Ravanan's Pushpakavimanam? We believe it can fly, don't we?

Velayudhan: But that's Ravanan, isn't it? He was something else. And he was a king. They can do whatever they want. Such people don't exist any more.

Geevarghese: We Christians don't believe in your Ravanan or his Pushpakavimanam. We are not supposed to...

That was the extent of our general knowledge. Kelan was the one and only social reformer in our part of the world. He built a school for the children from the marginal communities in our village. By school I mean just four posts with a handful of plaited palm leaves strung over as a roof. But the school remained closed for a long time because there was no one to teach the classes. Finally, I took over the responsibility of teaching. By teaching I mean just the alphabet and a bit of addition and subtraction. In those days, that is all teaching and learning amounted to in our back-of-beyond corner of the world.

Even after Valyammachi's death, Appan was troubled by his mother's godlessness. The Holy Bible says that parents will be punished for the sins of their children. Does it then also mean that children will be punished for the sins of their parents? Did God maintain a single, fat accounts register under the title 'Kottarathil Veedu', or did he have several smaller registers marked 'Kuncheriya' and 'Mathu' and 'Mathiri'? Appan preferred to believe that God had a smaller register titled 'Kuncheriya' in which he marked all his deeds, that only he got to enjoy the benefits of the God-fearing, prayerful life he led. Well, you can't blame him for thinking why he was doing all the hard work if the likes of me and Valyammachi who lived as we pleased were to receive the benefits.

I forgot to tell you about my marriage. Well, not much to say, really, except that it was the most foolish thing I ever did! Mariyamma was the first prospective bride I went to see. I didn't go to see her with any clear intention of getting married – I was bored, that's all. But when I saw her ... Oh my Lord! What a beautiful woman she was! I felt it would be a matter of great pride to be her husband. Thinking of it now, I feel bad for Mariyamma. So many hopes and dreams she would have brought with her when she came home as my bride at the tender age of fifteen...

On our first night together, I was anxious. What would I speak to her about? That's when I saw, amidst the clothes in her trunk, a picture of Geevarghese Sahada. You needn't have brought a picture of Geevarghese Sahada from home, I told her, all friendly-like, we have the same Geevarghese Sahada here. 'Oh no, you won't have *this* Geevarghese Sahada here,' she said with no sign that she was only a fifteen-year-old girl. 'This Geevarghese Sahada has been blessed by His Lordship.' By 'His Lordship' she meant the bishop who was a relative of hers. I felt like a fool, like I had been put in my place by a slip of a girl. What would I talk to her about now? I thought of all the things I knew about in my head. Toddy ... Toddy shop ... Kelan ... Kali ... Mathiri valyammachi ... Yes, that was it, I thought, Mathiri valyammachi would be a good topic, and would be a good match for her bishop.

'You know my grandmother, Mathiri valyammachi? She was a phenomenal woman,' I told her. 'Her main job was prophesying. And her prophecies always came true. I've often felt that it was she who decided on matters.'

'It is Our Lord Karthaveeshomishiha who decides on matters,' Mariyamma said gravely. 'If us puny humans try to decide matters, we will go straight to hell.'

That did it. I told her I had a headache and turned over and went to sleep. I was scared of that fifteen-year-old girl, I realized, in a way I had never felt before. I spent the next week at home, out of her way but at the same time not daring to go out, climbing into our bed and going to sleep before it was night. A desperate desire to see Valyammachi rose inside me.

By the end of that week, I felt like I didn't want to live any more. Gathering up my resolve, I went to the toddy shop and drank until I was plastered. Then I went to Valyammachi's grave, laid my head on her headstone and sobbed loudly.

'Geevarghese,' I heard her voice. 'Mariyamma understands the language of oppression more than the language of love. In any case, you too are more proficient in the language of oppression. This is how this relationship has been decided.'

I was doubtful, and I was reluctant to ill-treat such a young, beautiful woman. But since it was Valyammachi who said this, I decided to take her advice.

When I got home, Mariyamma was sitting in front of the photo of Geevarghese Sahada blessed by His Lordship, praying. I stomped on it and broke it into two pieces. Mariyamma looked at me, her eyes filled with fear. 'There is no need for another Geevarghese Sahada in this house,' I told her, looking straight into those eyes. 'There's a photo of him on the front veranda. Pray to it if you must.'

I have thought since, that Valyammachi could have given me better advice. Still, what can I say … from that day on, I found great satisfaction in scaring the bejesus out of Mariyamma.

By then, Mariyamma and my appan had become close beyond all belief. Well, between a husband like me and a mother-in-law like my ammachi, one cannot blame Mariyamma if she got the impression that my appan was a saint. They seemed content to spend hours chatting about the church and the clergy and His Lordship, the bishop. I overheard Mariyamma telling my appan that the next time the bishop visited her family, she would arrange for him to come to Kottarathil Veedu to meet Appan. Twenty years my appan waited for the bishop. And then he died – the bishop, not Appan.

Appan died many years after that. There will not be another human being on this earth who lived until the age of one hundred with the stubborn desire to go to heaven. I was seventy years old by the time I received even a portion of my inheritance. I wanted to cut off all the rubber and use the land for agriculture. But what agriculture was I to do at the age of seventy? My children have no interest in it. But Maria … do you know what she desires the most? To buy a lot of land and live on it, rearing animals and farming. Her greatest desire is to rear an elephant. She is the only one among my children and grandchildren who knows our family history and about our ancestors. She was always interested in learning those things, even when she was a mere child. But now … I wonder if it is my fault that she has turned out the way she has … I wonder if it was me who made her like this with stories of long-dead ancestors and whatnot…

# 8

# Chirammel Kathanar and the Family History of Kottarathil Veedu

'What is the point in living without knowing the history of your own family and your ancestors?' Geevarghese asked Little Maria. 'Have you ever heard your mama or your aunties and uncles mention Chirammel Kathanar?'

'Who is that?' asked Little Maria.

'Chirammel Kathanar was a priest who was a great-grandfather of ours, who lived eight or nine generations ago. It was he who taught Kadamattathu Kathanar, the renowned magician-priest, everything, except our kathanar did not become world famous like his student. Anyway, when the instruction was over, Chirammel Kathanar decided to test his student. He asked Kadamattathu Kathanar to loan him a gold chain. And every time Kadamattathu Kathanar asked for his chain back, Chirammel Kathanar would say, "Yes, yes, I'll return it immediately." Finally, fed up with the excuses, Kadamattathu

Kathanar came to our house to get his property back. But the moment he entered the house, Chirammel Kathanar shape-shifted into a gecko and escaped, and all Kadamattathu Kathanar saw was the swish of a vanishing tail. Pissed off, he cursed his guru: "May all your descendants be mad!"'

'And did anyone become mad?'

'Did they, ha! All this cursing and all, it's all nonsense, never takes effect.'

'And what happened to Chirammel Kathanar when he became a gecko?'

'Oh, he crawled away, and when he got to the ceiling of the kitchen, he saw that there was a plateful of steamed tapioca. So, he came down and ate his fill ... One time, in the middle of his sermon during Sunday Qurbana, Chirammel Kathanar produced a picture.

'"Do you know who this is?" he asked the congregation.

'"Our Lord Karthaveeshomishiha," said the believers.

'Chirammel Kathanar swung the picture this way and that a couple of times and held it up again.

'"So, who's this then?" he asked.

'Almost the entire population sat dumfounded, except for a handful who whispered: "Satan..."

'"So, how can we tell for sure who is who?" asked the Kathanar and continued with his sermon.

'One time, Kadamattathu Kathanar and Chirammel Kathanar were travelling together. When they began to feel hungry, they went to a nearby hovel in the hope of being given something to eat. But the people who lived there were very poor, and the woman told them sorrowfully that they had no rice and had not cooked a single meal in the last three days. "Don't you have even a broken piece of grain?" Kadamattathu Kathanar asked her, and when she said no, he asked her to check once again anyway. Irritated and muttering why they could not leave her alone even in her penury, the woman went off to look. After much searching, she found a piece of rice that was stuck to her winnow. "Here," she said, placing it into Kadamattathu Kathanar's palm, "boil it and eat it then." "Oh, this will do nicely," said the kathanar, trying to hide his embarrassment at being scolded. He then asked her to boil a pot of water. By then, she had no doubt that Kadamattathu Kathanar was unhinged. She did not think that of Chirammel Kathanar who had remained quiet all through this.

"'Some of us are dying of hunger here, and you think it's the time to joke around. Granted you're a priest and all, but I swear … you're testing my patience!"

'The thoroughly pissed off woman went and squatted in a corner of the hut, muttering to herself. So, Kadamattathu Kathanar filled a pot himself, boiled the water, put the tiny piece of broken rice in, and sat waiting, the boiling pot covered with a sliver of banana leaf. After some time, when they removed the leaf and looked inside … Lo and behold! A potful of super-fluffy rice, cooked to perfection! The woman gawped. But overcome with hunger, she sat right beside the kathanars and quickly began eating. And as soon as her hunger was under control, she went inside the house and came back with the bone of a dried fish.

'"Here," she said, handing it to Kadamattathu Kathanar. "Would be lovely to have a bit of dried-fish curry to go with the rice."

'Kadamattathu Kathanar became anxious because Chirammel Kathanar had not taught him the magic to create curry with dried fish. He gave his guru a troubled look. Stepping in at the time of need, Chirammel Kathanar had the curry made, and the three of them ate again. When it was time to leave, Chirammel Kathanar broke his silence.

'"Don't sit around expecting a similar miracle tomorrow also," he said to the woman. "We only do these tricks when we are hungry."

'As they walked away, Kadamattathu Kathanar said, "That was unnecessary. You didn't have to upset her."

'To which Chirammel Kathanar replied, "I was only warning her so that she will not nurture unrealistic expectations."

'So, as you can see, Maria, there are many such stories about our ancestor Chirammel Kathanar, but no one is aware of them.' Geevarghese concluded the storytelling session.

They were wandering around the compound. Ayyappan, who was picking black pepper from the vines smiled at them. He was a silent type of person. Geevarghese told Little Maria that Ayyappan used to be a chatterbox before the Emergency. It was the slogan 'Navadakkoo paniyedukkoo' – control your tongue and carry on with your work – that changed him. Fearing that the police would arrest him if he spoke unless it was absolutely necessary, and at the same time unable to define what 'work' entailed exactly, he gave up speaking altogether even when he was at home. Was putting up a fence around one's own house work? Or was it work only if one did it in exchange for wages? The dilemma transformed Ayyappan into Mookanayyappan – Silent Ayyappan.

'Ayyappa, there's no need to exert yourself without rest,' Geevarghese, who had no interest in seeing money accumulating in Kuncheriya's cash box, told him. 'This is not the Emergency any more.'

Using the word 'emergency' wherever he could, whether it was necessary or not, had become a habit for Geevarghese. But Ayyappan barely heard what he said, engrossed as he was in his work. No one could tell when the police would arrive, after all!

'Appacha, why do they let pepper vines climb up coconut trees?' Maria wanted to know.

'Well, let's say a coconut tree brings in an income of a hundred rupees. But a coconut tree with a pepper vine clambering all over it brings in five hundred rupees. That is the economics of it.'

Chandippatti ran into their path in the company of a female in the throes of lust.

'Appacha, look, Chandippatti is climbing over that other dog and trying to kill it!' Maria shouted. 'Chandi! Get off!'

Geevarghese picked up a stone and threw it at the dogs, but the female, with the natural reflex of street dogs, deftly avoided it and ran away. It was Chandi who got hit.

'Doing the dirty in front of the child!' Geevarghese admonished. 'Get lost, you scoundrel!'

Chandi turned back with his usual response at the tip of his tongue – 'This is the trouble with you humans!' – but seeing Geevarghese pick up another stone, he ran away quickly.

'Geevarghese nanaar talks to the dog as though it is a human being!' Ayyappan muttered involuntarily.

# 9

# Maria's Social Life

With his round, pumpkin eyes and a mouth that watered enough to sink a ship, seven-year-old Kuttappayi strolled back and forth in front of Geevarghese's shop. Every time he thought of the Parry's and Nutrine candies inside the shop, saliva dripped from the corners of his mouth. Maria, meanwhile, was inside the shop, her stomach hurting from all the sweets she had scoffed. Grabbing a handful of sweets, the other hand pressed against her aching tummy, Maria stepped outside. She had, after all, decided that she would marry Kuttappayi when they were all grown up.

Kuttappayi was the son of one of their servants, Sumathi. He was, at this tender age, already efficient at climbing the tallest of the trees and catching the largest of the fish in the canal. He was always around, flitting across Maria's field of vision. He did not have to go to school. Above all else, Maria thought Kuttappayi with his very dark skin was the most beautiful human being in the world.

Little Maria stood in front of Kuttappayi and held out the handful of candies a little bashfully. Kuttappayi extended his hand in turn but pulled it back at the last minute.

'I don't have any money,' he said.

'I don't want your money,' Maria said. 'Just pick me some ainippazham.' She loved those wild jackfruits, but they grew on very tall trees.

'No, I don't want them, girl. Your appachan will scold me.'

Granted Kuttappayi was the boy she was going to marry, but Maria did not like the way he called her 'girl'.

'My name is not *girl*. My name is Maria.'

Steeped in the misery of having to see the Parry's and Nutrine up close and yet having to say no, Kuttappayi did not respond. Maria could not hold on to her irritation for too long either. So, she held the sweets out to him again.

'Appachan said I can sell these to you in exchange for ainippazham. You know, barter, like they do in Raghavan's shop.'

Now that was reasonable. Kuttappayi, who obviously did not know that Maria's appachan had said no such thing, could get on board with that. He grabbed the sweets, said, 'I'll bring the ainippazham in the evening, girl,' over his shoulder, and flitted away. Maria was hoping to chat with him for some more time, but all she could do was stand there bereft.

When Maria returned to the shop, Josootty was complaining about Kuncheriya who had called him names. Geevarghese tried to console him, saying that his father was a mad person and that we should forgive mad people for what they say.

'Appacha, how do we recognize mad people?' Maria asked after listening to their conversation for a while. 'I would have never guessed Kuncheriya valyappachan was mad until you told me.'

'We have to observe them closely and carefully,' said Geevarghese, 'only then we'll begin to see that there is something not quite right there. Those who behave totally normally – some of them are mad. In fact, they are the ones who are properly mad.'

'Are you mad, Appacha?'

'Ey, what sort of foolish question is that!'

'What about Ammachi?'

'Well, only those who have a certain level of intelligence can go mad. There should be some space for the madness to operate, isn't it?'

'Anna valyamma says that Shoshamma valyammachi was totally mad.'

'Hm ... to be clear, though, my mother's madness was a manifestation of her wickedness. No brain can tolerate such high-quality wickedness.'

As the conversation progressed, Kali's daughter Thanka came into the shop for some coconut oil. Maria, who was scared of her, quickly slid behind Geevarghese. One time, when Thanka had picked up dried twigs of rubber from Kuncheriya's plantation, Maria had told her off. 'Who are you to stop me? Do these belong to your father?' Thanka had asked in retaliation. Maria should have said yes, but instead she had run away, suddenly finding herself tongue-tied. Since then, she had been scared of Thanka.

'A hundred milli coconut oil,' Thanka said, handing the bottle to Geevarghese. Then, spotting the lurking Maria, she continued. 'Can't you return this child to her parents, Nanaarey? You'll spoil her, no doubt about that.'

Geevarghese poured some of the oil back into the drum. 'I was about to give you a hundred and twenty milli of oil, only because you are Kali's daughter. But now that you've opened your mouth and said that, I'm not going to.'

'You should have given her ninety milli,' Maria said after she left. 'Pattithanka!'

Kelan walked into the shop. 'I just saw Thanka. What's she muttering about?'

'Impertinence, what else!' said Geevarghese.

'Still ... she's our Kali's daughter, isn't she, Nanaarey?'

A deep sigh followed Kelan's words. Geevarghese and Velayudhan sighed with him. Maria and Josootty did not sigh because they did not know Kali.

Leaving Josootty to look after the shop, the rest of them set out to the toddy shop. Maria jumped into the puddles left by the recent rain and splashed water everywhere. Velayudhan joined her until the water he splashed fell on Geevarghese's body, which put an end to the game. Kelan told Maria that rain was the piss water of the gods. He had no way of knowing that Maria would believe it for the rest of her life.

At the toddy shop, Geevarghese ordered tapioca, beef ularthiyathu and fish curry. Soon, the buzz of toddy coursed through their veins.

'Child, you're the one who should keep alive your appachan's legacy,' Velayudhan said, pouring a little toddy in a glass for Maria.

Kelan began talking about the misery the people had endured during the Emergency. 'You people's Indira Gandhi arrested so many people and put them in jail,' he said. 'So much cruelty she did...'

No one quite knew who Kelan meant when he said 'you people'. As far as he was concerned, it involved everyone other than him. Velayudhan was the one who replied, taking on the responsibility of representing 'you people'.

'Ey ... I don't believe she did or would do such terrible things,' he said. 'After all, she is the daughter of our Mahatma Gandhi, isn't she?'

'Indira Gandhi is not Mahatma Gandhi's daughter, you idiot,' Geevarghese corrected him. 'She's Nehru's daughter.'

Velayudhan could not stomach that. As Kelan continued arguing with his opponents, he sat there, perplexed.

'What kind of foolishness is that!' Velayudhan said eventually. 'Why would they give Gandhi's name to Nehru's daughter? They might be close friends and all, but that doesn't make it right. Now, Geevarghese nanaarey, you and I are close friends. But that doesn't mean I can name my daughter Saudamini Geevarghese!'

In those days, a key subject that was discussed in toddy shops all across the land was Skylab. It was widely known that this American artificial satellite orbiting the earth was about to fall out of the sky. Everyone was absolutely certain that it was headed for our land. The idea terrified most people, but there were those who felt an abiding pride in the fact that an American satellite had chosen our land, even if it was to explode all over it. There were constant announcements over the radio cautioning listeners to be on the alert, but they did not say how to be alert. Christians went to church en masse to partake in the sacrament of confession. Some people went to their relatives' houses in faraway places hoping to escape Skylab, but to their surprise, wherever they went, people in those places were as scared as they were, convinced that the satellite was headed right towards them.

Kelan used the opportunity to score political points. 'Don't you see now?' he said to all the anti-communists in the area. 'Don't you see what your ally is doing? No Indian would ever have anything to fear from a satellite that belonged to the Soviet Union!' Velayudhan, meanwhile, was more calculating. He moved out of his hut with his wife Devaki, and began living in his yard, praying to all the gods he could think of that at least a teensiest piece of Skylab would fall on his hut. 'Then I can receive compensation from the Americans,' he told everyone at the toddy shop. There were rumours that American newspapers would reward anyone who took them even a tiny piece of Skylab hundreds of thousands of dollars. Velayudhan began dreaming of the palace he would build in the place where his hut stood now.

However, to the utmost disappointment of Velayudhan and the huge relief of his compatriots, Skylab went and fell somewhere in Australia. In those days, Australia was not as famous as it is now. In any case, everyone felt somewhat dejected after it was all over. They would have liked the Skylab episode and the excitement it brought to continue for a little longer.

A panchayat-owned road cut through the middle of Kottarathil Veedu's compound. Maria played 'bus driving' sitting on top of a cashew tree by its side. She did not know that it had grown from the seed her appachan's friend Kali had planted. The bus in Maria's game was 'Shinestar' that plied from Koothattukulam to Ernakulam. Maria's main role was that of the driver Kuriakose, but she also took on the roles of the conductor Babychettan who wrote out the tickets as well as the two young men, Shine and Bose, who were the 'kilis' – cleaners and general busybodies who oversaw the getting in and out of passengers. The tickets were pages of a notebook torn to small pieces on which she scribbled with a pencil. As she stopped the bus to let people in, she would call out: 'Move along inside, brother, there's enough space to play football in there.'

As she pulled into the bus stop calling out 'Ernaalam … Ernaalam…', she felt the presence of someone watching her. She looked down, and there was Kuttappayi, staring into her bus with his pumpkin eyes, one hand clamped over his laughing mouth and the other holding a small basket of ainippazham. The reason Maria loved playing in the cashew tree was that she could spot

Kuttappayi coming from a distance. But that day, busy as she was with letting people in and out of the bus, she had forgotten to watch out for him. To be perfectly clear, it wasn't that she had forgotten to watch out. He was late and Maria, bored from waiting, had begun to play her game and got distracted. And now, there he was!

As it is, Maria felt shy in Kuttappayi's presence, and now that he had caught her immersed in her game, she felt mortified. Kuttappayi realized Maria had seen him laugh, so he composed himself. 'Here's the ainippazham, girl,' he said, placing the little reed basket on the floor. Then he flitted away. Every time he flitted along that road, he would look up into the branches of the cashew tree. He knew Maria would be sitting in it, but he did not know that she was sitting there waiting for him.

# 10

# A Day in the Life of Little Maria in Kottarathil Veedu

After Geevarghese, the person Little Maria liked the most in Kottarathil Veedu was her aunty, Sheena. Sheenanty knew a lot of things, and because of her and her radio, Atal Bihari Vajpayee, Chandra Shekhar and George Fernandes were as familiar to Maria as Mathachan valyappan, Thomachan chachan and Kuncheriya valyappachan. And when Sheenanty lost her radio, it was Maria who was more upset.

Even Geevarghese liked the radio Sheena brought home one day, but the new, unfamiliar object vexed Kuncheriya no end. The voices coming out of it made him feel that disembodied spirits were gliding around the house blathering on in a cacophony of languages. Finally, when he could stand it no more, he took it and threw it out. It landed in the yard and continued to make noises. So, Kuncheriya picked it up and put it in the pond, ensuring, thus, that it would never speak again.

Sheena was in charge of Maria's studies. Truth be told, Maria's studies really didn't amount to much. As Mariyamma would say, after gallivanting around the toddy shop and the market with Geevarghese, the child barely had time to study.

When Maria was old enough to go to school, there was some confusion about her future. Susanna and Neena argued strongly that Maria should be returned to her parents. Maria's papa was also of this opinion, if only because he did not like the idea of being indebted to his in-laws. Susanna's opinion was that it was the responsibility of the parents to bring up a child. For her, a child was not a 'he' or a 'she' or a person of any kind, but an 'it', a thing, and that thing, she argued, would be spoiled if it wasn't brought up by its parents. And the best evidence to support her argument was Maria herself, who was already three-quarters spoiled. Neena wanted Maria returned to her parents for entirely personal reasons. The child meddled in everything and was a threat to her privacy.

On the opposite side of this argument were Geevarghese, Mariyamma and Sheena. Geevarghese promised that he would stop dragging Maria along on his wanderings the moment she started school. 'Such betrayal,' Maria told Chandippatti, and he agreed that he would never have expected Geevarghese to exhibit such hypocrisy. But when Geevarghese explained that if he hadn't made that promise, her parents would have taken her back home, Maria was pacified. Even Chandi had to admit that it was a very clever move.

Maria's mama, Anna, was not in a hurry to have Maria returned to her because she already had three other children to look after at home – Anne, Mathew and Lisa. The third, Lisa, was not even meant to be born, but she came out looking like a carbon copy of Anna! That and the fact that she was the youngest made her the favourite of her mother. Anne and Mathew were already favourites – Anne, by virtue of being the firstborn, and Mathew because he was the only boy. With nothing special to recommend her, Maria's position in the family was uncertain.

'How am I supposed to look after Maria too?' Anna protested.

No one asked Maria's opinion. If they had, she would have told them, in no uncertain terms, that she did not want to live in the family of those wretched children.

Soon, the decision was made: Maria would live in Kottarathil Veedu for some more time.

In addition to taking care of Maria's studies, Sheena also did things like buying her snacks and telling her stories. As soon as she was home from her trip to the toddy shop with her grandfather, Maria would follow Sheenanty, pleading for a story. Here is one of Sheenanty's stories:

> *Once, there were two woodcutters – Ramu and Shyamu. They were friends, but Ramu was a decent man while Shyamu was crooked. They cut wood in a forest on the banks of a river. One day, as Ramu was cutting wood, his axe fell into the river. What would he do now? It was with the money he made from cutting firewood that he looked after his family. Upset at the loss of his livelihood, Ramu sat on the bank and began crying. Moved by his sorrow, the River Goddess appeared in front of him.*
>
> *'What happened, son? Why are you crying?' she asked.*
>
> *'My axe fell into the river, O Goddess of mine,' Ramu said.*
>
> *The River Goddess decided to test him. She disappeared for a while and reappeared with an axe made of gold in her hand.*
>
> *'Is this your axe, son?'*
>
> *'No, Goddess. Cutting wood with a gold axe? That would be silly, wouldn't it?'*

*The Goddess disappeared again and came back up, this time with a silver axe.*

*'Bet this is the one.'*

*'No. I don't know any woodcutter who would cut wood with gold and silver axes.'*

*Finally, the Goddess showed him an iron axe.*

*'This must be it then.'*

*'Yes, my dear Goddess! Yes, this is my axe!'*

*'I'm pleased with you, son,' the Goddess said. 'You're a good man, and as a reward for your honesty, you can have these gold and silver axes as well.'*

*'Am I to cut wood with the gold axe from now on?' asked Ramu, perplexed.*

*'No, silly! Sell these two axes and put the money in the bank. Or start some business with it and live as a rich man. What else!'*

*And thus, Ramu became a rich man. When Shyamu asked him how he managed to do that, Ramu told him the entire story.*

*So, the next day, Shyamu went to the forest by the river and began cutting wood. But try as he might, his axe would not fall into the river. Fed up, he threw it in the river and began wailing at the top of his voice. The River Goddess appeared and asked him what happened, and Shyamu told her about his lost axe.*

*The Goddess disappeared into the river and came back up with a gold axe.*

*'Is this your axe?'*

*'Yes, oh yes, my dear Goddess! That is my axe. Now, the other day, my silver axe fell in the river. If you could fetch that one also for me, I'd be much obliged.'*

*'Oh yeah? Who do you think you're talking to? Do you know how long I've been keeping these gold and silver axes for the express purpose of testing people's honesty? And now I'm not going to return your iron axe to you either. Liar!'*

*'What am I supposed to do then without my axe?'* asked Shyamu.

*'Go buy another axe. I don't care!'*

*And with that the Goddess disappeared.*

'So, do you see what happens when we tell lies?' Sheena asked, concluding the story.

'But Sheenanty, it was the Goddess who told lies first,' protested Little Maria. 'To test the woodcutters.'

'Gods are allowed to test our honesty,' Sheena told her. 'It's based on these tests that they decide whether we should go to heaven or to hell.'

Whenever Sheena told Maria stories, Geevarghese hid somewhere nearby and listened to them. The story of the fox that fell into a vat of blue dye was his favourite.

That night, Maria dreamt of Karthav Eesho Mishiha playing a game, throwing gold, silver and iron axes into a river and picking them up again. He seemed to be thoroughly enjoying Himself. Suddenly, a blue whale, wandering into the river from the ocean by mistake, swallowed the gold and silver axes and swam back into the ocean. The next time, when Karthav dived into the water for the gold axe, He came up with the iron one. Confused, He stared at it, decided that He had made a mistake, and dived again for the silver axe. But when He came up, there it was again, the iron axe! He tried diving again and again into the river water, but all He could come up with was the iron axe! When Mariyamma shook

Little Maria awake the next morning, she was still watching the confounded Karthav diving into the water and coming up again, searching fruitlessly for the gold and silver axes.

'Poor Karthav,' Maria sighed.

'What's that, my dear?'

'Oh, nothing, Ammachi.'

When Maria stepped out on to the veranda, her appachan and Kuncheriya valyappachan were sitting on their respective easy chairs, drinking black coffee. Anna valyamma was cleaning her teeth with chaff ash and a mango leaf. Her teeth, even at this age, stood white and shiny like sturdy little soldiers, all because of, according to her, this regular routine. But ever since the dementia had gotten hold of her, Anna valyamma would clean her teeth with whatever leaf she could find, including leaves of jackfruit, guava and kozhivalan, the amaranth with its rooster-tail flowers. That was the one good thing about dementia – you were released from having to do certain things in certain ways; you could do anything any which way.

Sheenanty was reading one half of the newspaper while Thomachan chachan read the other half. Ammachi was in the kitchen, making appam for breakfast, ably assisted by Eetha, while Eetha herself was being assisted by her daughter, Molly. Chirutha was sweeping the yard, and Chandippatti followed her making the tidy yard untidy again. This was the Kottarathil Veedu that greeted Maria when she woke up and walked into the morning of a new day. The first thing she did was to go see Chandippatti.

'I've never seen a dog like this one right here,' Chirutha began as soon as she saw Maria. 'Like it is possessed by the devil himself! What else will make a dog so contrary? Child, tell your appachan to get rid of this thing and get a proper dog, an Alsatian. Haven't you seen Ouseph nanaar's dog? So brave! So obedient! Leave a plate of chicken curry in front of it, and it won't touch it until someone says, "Eat, Kaiser." That dog will die if it sees this silly thing here, ashamed that this is a dog too!'

Listening to her, Chandippatti died laughing. He told Maria that an Alsatian was not a real dog. That honour went to local mongrels like him. Maria did not hear the rest of what he said because she ran to Ammachi who had been calling her to come and brush her teeth.

'Child, don't forget what I said about the Alsatian,' Chirutha called after her as she rushed off.

Although she was unsure of its purpose, Maria had to brush her teeth every morning. She had a small red toothbrush and a tube of Binaca toothpaste. The toothpaste came with little plastic toy animals – yellow monkey, blue lion, violet giraffe, orange fish, green dinosaur … Maria loved those little animals and waited impatiently for the toothpaste tube to empty so that a new one could be bought. Sometimes, her impatience got the better of her, and she aided the process by secretly squeezing the paste out of the tube.

One time, Ittan, who did the grocery shopping, had come back with a toothpaste named Cibaca. He said that the company had changed its name – as though the BIN had caused bad luck and they had replaced it with CIB. Maria did not like the new toothpaste that had no plastic animals in the packet.

When Maria went in after brushing her teeth, Kuncheriya and Geevarghese were already at the dining table. As usual, a pile of six appams and chicken curry made with roasted and ground masala sat in the plates in front of Kuncheriya. Geevarghese ate his appam dipped in sugar – he loved eating sugar with everything, and sometimes put a spoonful of sugar in his palm and walked around licking it. Sheenanty had already left for college, and Neenanty was shut in her room as usual. Thomachan chachan ate later as he had all the time in the world. Anna valyamma had placed herself in front of the fire in the yard with a potful of water. In her dementia-gripped mind, she was boiling water for Shoshamma chedathi's bath. Three times the pot boiled dry and she had Eetha refill it. After the third time, she scrambled up. 'I am such a fool,' she said. 'Shoshamma chedathi has been dead for so many years!'

Mariyamma followed Maria, trying to make her eat the freshly made appam.

'I don't want it, Ammachi, I'm not hungry,' said Maria.

'I don't know what's wrong with this child. She's not been eating properly for days now. She's been eating out?' Mariyamma began as a statement, but it ended as a question aimed at Geevarghese.

'Ey, nothing,' Geevarghese protested. 'She says no to everything I try to give her.'

'Ammachi, I'm not hungry because every night I eat cake in my dreams.'

In those days, of Geevarghese's children, only Sheena, Thomachan and Neena lived at home. Shajan was away studying medicine. Thomachan, lazy by birth, gave up his studies after Class 10, and gave up all thoughts of doing anything with his life. Whenever Mariyamma brought up the topic of a job, he brushed it away saying that he had no intention of making his life more complicated. He spent his time reading only the Congress-friendly reports and news items in the newspapers and magazines Sheena bought. When he was old enough, he got married to the youngest daughter from a family that only had two daughters and no sons, and went to live with them. His wife's family had only good things to say about their son-in-law who never went out and spent all his time at home.

As for Neena ... as Maria says, it is better not to say anything about Neenanty. She spent the entire day in her room with the doors locked. Maria could not stand Neenanty, and the feeling was reciprocated with equal intensity.

'Appacha, why is Neenanty sitting in that room all the time with the doors locked?' Maria complained to Geevarghese. 'Tell her to open the door. I want to play with the big box in that room.'

'Neena...' Geevarghese called, banging on the door. The moment she heard her father's voice, Neena opened the door fearfully.

'If you lock this door again, there won't be a door to lock any more,' threatened Geevarghese.

Neena glared at Maria, but Maria ignored her and went straight to the big wooden chest. First, she took on the role of Chirammel Kathanar. Then she also became Kadamattathu Kathanar.

Ka. Ka: 'Chirammel Kathanar, I'm going to hide in this box. I challenge you to open it by the time I count to one hundred.'

Chi. Ka: 'Ha ha ha! You won't reach ten. I'll have it opened by then. Ha ha ha!'

Ka. Ka: 'Impossible! Ha ha ha! I'm a better magician than you are. I know more tricks, other tricks that you haven't taught me. If you lose, you will give me your gold chain as reward. Agreed?'

Chi. Ka: 'Stop jabbering, you fool, and get on with it. Ha ha ha! Shut the box.'

Kadamattathu Kathanar shut the box. Chirammel Kathanar pretended to be reciting some mantra and began counting. One, two, three, four, five, six, seven, eight, nine ... Before he counted ten, Chirammel Kathanar opened the box and looked at Kadamattathu Kathanar.

Chi. Ka: 'Ha ha ha!'

Kadamattathu Kathanar was livid, his face red with embarrassment and anger.

Ka. Ka: 'When did you learn how to open the box? You didn't know it before…'

Chi. Ka: 'Ha ha ha! It was my granddaughter Maria who taught me this trick. She is the greatest magician in the whole wide world. Ha ha ha!'

'For the love of God! Stop with your ha ha ha already!' Neena screamed. 'This stupid child … Get out of my room! Scram!'

Maria let out a 'Ha ha ha ha ha ha' that shook the entire Kottarathil Veedu and left the room.

'Chirammel Kathanar, get rid of Neenanty, kill her,' she whispered as she walked out. 'Or, at the very least, break one of her legs.'

# 11

# Kuncheriya's Doubts and Dilemmas About Heaven

Anna looked for Kuncheriya all around the house, from morning till night. She ran into him several times, but she did not recognize him. And the few times she did recognize him, she forgot she was looking for him.

At one point, she stopped Maria and asked her, 'Who are you, child?'

'I'm Maria, Anna valyamma,' Maria said.

'And whose daughter are you?'

'Anna's.'

'Anna's? But I am Anna. I don't have any children.'

Surprised and confused, she went looking for Kuncheriya again.

'Did you hear, Chetta,' Anna said when she found Kuncheriya. 'That Thresya from Plachottil house ... she died.'

'How old was she, do you know?' asked Kuncheriya.

'Must be eighty, eighty-five. There was a proposal for you to marry her. You remember? But you said no. Too dark, you said.'

'I didn't say she was too dark. I said she had a squint.'

'Ah, it's all the same.'

Anna kept on talking. Watching her wrinkled face, Kuncheriya felt that his ninety-odd-year-long life was too short. He realized, with a slight sense of surprise, that he had never been able to love this woman even though they had spent so many years in the same house. Come to think of it, he had not been able to love his wife either. Was that his fault? Or was it hers?

Kuncheriya's biggest fear was that his inability to love those near and dear to him would turn out to be a problem for his eventual entry into heaven. He had spent these long ninety-odd years on this earth with the sole purpose of attaining heaven after death. And it wasn't that he had never faced other temptations along the way, but the temptation of heaven was too strong to be swayed by any of them.

From a young age, he had cultivated good relationships with the church and the clergy. He donated a large part, well, at least a not inconsiderable part, of his income to the church. 'Why give all this money to these poor priests?' Geevarghese would ask each time a donation was made and a receipt was being written out. 'Why not line your coffin with it and take it straight to Karthaveeshomishiha?' Kuncheriya's tongue would throb, wanting to give him a cutting reply, but he would refrain. Having his name entered into Karthav's account book was an auspicious moment. Why take the risk of swearing at his son and having it stricken off?

In addition to the donations, Kuncheriya hedged his bets by committing to memory the Holy Bible, the book that promised to ease the journey to heaven.

Still, Kuncheriya had his doubts. He tried with all his might to suppress them, but they floated to the top often. For instance, was it right that Karthav cursed the fig tree for the sole reason that it couldn't bear fruit? And why did He make the rich man's entry into heaven – even when the man in question was a good man – so difficult? With the exception of these moments of doubt, Kuncheriya submitted himself entirely to the church, to Karthav Eesho Mishiha, and to the priests who were His representatives on earth.

His wife, Shoshamma, was never able to satisfy his body or his soul, and yet Kuncheriya never strayed, never thought of another woman. Not because he was afraid of Shoshamma but because he was afraid of God. Many were the occasions when he felt the overwhelming urge to bash her head open, but he controlled himself only because of the fear of God. Whenever these thoughts came up in his mind, he hoped, prayed, that Karthav was too busy with other concerns to pay attention to what he was up to.

Despite all this, Kuncheriya was terrified of death. His place in heaven was ninety per cent guaranteed, but he was loath to let go of the pleasures of earth. It was Geevarghese who had a clear understanding of his feelings. What attracted Kuncheriya to heaven was the absence of hell. But that didn't necessarily mean heaven was better than earth. Kuncheriya did not quite understand what was so good about having the opportunity to sit in the laps of Abraham, Isahaq and Yakub. The whole set-up made him think of a nursery school where a bunch of old men and women sat around together. Kuncheriya was certain that a heaven without meat curry and fried fish would be entirely joyless, meaningless, and he prayed fervently that there would be tasty food and moderate hunger, just enough of the feeling to make the food desirable, in heaven.

Thus, towards the end of his life, Kuncheriya lived in a constant state of anxiety over death, heaven and hell. He was destined to live in this state for another decade, for it wasn't until he was a hundred years old that Kuncheriya finally died.

# 12
# Anne, Mathew, Lisa ... and Maria

'Ammachi, those kids are coming with their mother.'
'What kids?'
'That Anne, Mathew and Lisa.'
'They are your siblings, aren't they, Maria? You shouldn't call them "those kids"...'
'Well, I don't like those kids ... I don't like their papa and I don't like their mama!'

Anne, dressed in an orange frock, was the one to enter the house first, followed by Mathew in a pair of khaki trousers and red-and-black chequered shirt. Behind him was Anna in a violet sari printed with peacock feathers, and hanging from her fingertips, Lisa, looking like a little angel in a pink frock. As though to demonstrate to Maria how loving she could be towards well-behaved children, Neena gathered Lisa into her arms and began talking weird baby-talk to her: 'Dudududu ... dududu ... dududududu...'

It was only after they sat down and had a cup of tea – accompanied by achappam and avalosunda – that Anna noticed Little Maria.

'Ammachi, why on earth is this child walking around naked?'

Maria was dressed only in her C for Cat knickers. Ever since they arrived, she had been trying really hard to show off the knickers to Anne, Mathew and Lisa, to attract their attention and make them jealous. The knickers had a picture of a cat sprawled on a carpet with the words 'C for Cat' written on it. Although it was sleepy, the cat had its head up and was keeping a careful watch on what was going on around it.

But no one seemed to be interested…

Fed up, Maria sidled up to Lisa.

'I have others like this too – one with A for Apple and another with B for Ball,' she said. 'Did you see this cat?'

Lisa was more interested in the live cat under the chair, and ignored her.

'Tell me, why is this child naked?' Anna repeated her question.

It was Neena who answered. 'That's her new game, chechi, ever since Sheena bought her those knickers. Showing off the cat to everyone who passes by.'

Maria followed Lisa, trying to show her the cat, but Lisa continued ignoring her. Not very pretty, that frock of hers, Maria thought, and moved closer to Lisa to feel the lace between her fingers. Then, she gave it a tug. It tore, and Lisa began bawling at the top of her voice: 'My angel frock…' Anna gave Maria a slap which set Maria bawling at the top of *her* voice.

'Podee patti!' she screamed at Anna. 'You're not my mama. My ammachi is my mama … I hate youuuu!'

The frock episode came to an end when the other, older, Anna entered the room.

'Ah, who's this? Susanna? When did you arrive?'

Anna did not bother correcting Anna valyamma. What would be the point, lost as she was with the dementia affecting her memory. Besides, her own child had just called her a bitch in front of everyone and told her she was not her mother!

'We just got here, Valyamma,' she said instead.

'How many children do you have?'

'Four.'

'But you brought only three with you, eh?'

Anna began to get angry. 'Are you blind? Can't you see four of them standing right here?'

'Aha! This one here, this is your child, is it?' Anna valyamma asked with a surprised look on her face. 'Every time I ask her, she says she's Anna's daughter.' She turned to Maria. 'Child, your mama's name is not Anna. It's Susanna. Children these days!'

When the tears and sniffling from the frock episode ended, Maria stepped out into the yard. Anne and Mathew were playing ball – with the ball Appachan had bought for her at the church festival! The sight was very upsetting, but Maria stood there taking time to think through what to do. Every time her siblings came to visit, Maria fell out with them, quarrelled with them, and on each occasion, she received a good thrashing from Anna, Neena, Sheena and even Mariyamma. On this visit, she had already been thrashed by Anna. It was only when they came home that Maria got punished in this way. And, of course, at school where it was a festival of thrashing. Maria was not at all interested in being beaten by Anna again, but what to do, her anger towards Anne, Mathew and Lisa was more than she could control.

So, when Mathew threw the ball at Anne, Maria jumped in and caught it. They told her to give it back. She refused. Then ensued a tussle for possession which soon escalated into bites and scratches and pushes. Finally, Ammachi came out, broke a switch off the tamarind tree and thrashed Maria left and right. She did not thrash Anne and Mathew. They were guests who only visited occasionally. Besides, it was Maria who was always doing something naughty.

Swearing that she would hate Anne, Mathew, Lisa and their papa and mama for her entire life, Maria went looking for Chandippatti. In Chandi's opinion, Maria was jealous of Anne, Mathew and Lisa because they were fairer and prettier than Maria and had better clothes than her. They did not gallivant about the place eating thondippazham and chethippazham from the bushes; they ate oranges and apples bought from the shops.

Despite his proclivity for making such lofty proclamations, Chandippatti landed himself every now and then in comical and foolish situations that made everyone laugh. This was one such occasion, and here is what happened.

One afternoon, Chandi was taking a shit in the middle of a narrow lane when an old Yezdi came that way. Chandi was not meant to be in that lane at that moment. He had been waiting outside the toddy shop for Geevarghese so that they could go fetch Maria from school. At that moment, a mongrel bitch, never before seen in that area, came dancing by past where he was sprawled, and went on its way, still dancing. Who was this female who went past totally ignoring a fulsome male dog, Chandi wanted to know, and he got up and followed her, but she had disappeared! He searched all over the place in vain and was returning to the toddy shop when he felt like taking a shit.

Chandi could have moved to the side quite easily and made way for the motorbike. He had not begun doing his business and was only getting himself into a conducive position. Besides, it was dogs who were supposed to make way for vehicles, not the other way round. But Chandi stood his ground, glaring at the men on the motorbike with a disdainful expression on his face never before seen in a dog. Perhaps it was the conviction that he was a prestigious person, and a member of the most prestigious family in the area to boot, that made Chandi do what he did.

The problem was this: The men on the motorbike were outsiders who had no idea of Chandippatti's fame. They were on their way to a house to give them news of a death. Has anyone ever heard of the news of a death being delayed because the bearers of the news had to wait until a dog finished taking a shit? As the motorbike neared Chandi, the man riding pillion bent over, picked up a stone and, with a cry of 'Look at the dirty mongrel's impertinence!', threw it at him.

Chandippatti, who moved through life mostly immersed in himself, did not have the ready reflex that was common to dogs in general. So, he did not know how to avoid the stone and it hit him in the face. Chandi's first impulse was to run home and lie in the pile of ash in the yard, but he could not. Why should he do what ordinary dogs did? Was there really any use in lying quietly in a pile of ash when hurt? Caught in these dilemmas, Chandi went around for days with his face all puffed up. Even in those days, the question that was foremost in his mind was this: 'How the hell did that mongrel bitch disappear like that?'

You have heard the saying 'Like the man who was struck by lightning getting bitten by a snake…' This incident was like that as far as Chandippatti was concerned – one disaster on top of another – because he was already suffering from an intense toothache. He was gnawing on a piece of granite as usual to sharpen his teeth when suddenly there was a piercing pain in his right molar. He ignored the pain at first – he was, after all, a very brave dog – but by the next day, Chandi began to howl. The pain was too intense, and on top of it was the biting hunger from not being able to eat anything. Finally, Geevarghese and Maria took him to the vet in town. The doctor told them that it was the first time in the whole world that toothache was reported in a dog. The teeth of animals were made to suit the type of food they ate, so despite never brushing them, they never had toothache.

Later, whenever she thought of Chandi standing there looking miserably at the doctor, Maria would burst out laughing. The doctor looked at Chandi and said: 'Aaa...' Chandi did not understand what he was saying and stood there gawping. So, Maria opened her mouth wide, and said, 'Chandi, look, like this ... aaa ... aaa aaa ... aaa...' Chandi got it, and opened his mouth. The doctor employed the various tools at his disposal – pliers, scissors, knife, spanner – and examined his mouth. Whenever his mouth was free of tools, Chandi resumed howling. Finally, the doctor pulled a tooth out. Maria looked at it. It was rotten! Unable to stand the pain, Chandi ran out and ate some mud. As they were leaving, the doctor gave them a tube of toothpaste.

'It's a foreign brand, imported to brush the teeth of pedigree dogs. There really is no need for any dog to brush its teeth. But some people like to do it to show off how special their dogs are. It will be the first time a mongrel will be using toothpaste and brushing its teeth!'

From the very next day, Maria began brushing Chandi's teeth more diligently and regularly than she brushed her own.

There was, in actual fact, a reason behind Chandi's toothache. The orange Nutrine sweet in Geevarghese's shop was something Chandi could not resist, and he often begged Maria to give him some. He would eat them, and imitating Maria, would hang his orange-stained tongue out, saying, 'Aaa ... aaa...' But the funny part was that Chandi called the orange Nutrine 'green sweet'. So, Maria would give him the green Parry's.

'Not this one,' Chandi would say. 'Give me the green one.'

'This is the green one, Chandi.'

'No, you idiot. This is orange. Give me the other one there, the green one.' And he would touch the jar of Nutrine.

'Oh, this silly Chandi,' Maria would think and give him the Nutrine. Soon, she learned to give him the sweets he wanted, whenever he wanted them. The only problem was that, when they asked, 'What colour are leaves?' in the school exam, Maria answered, 'Orange.'

Maria asked Shajan chachan why Chandi referred to the colour orange as green. He gave her a matter-of-fact answer. (By this, it is meant that Shajan did not address the part where Maria said 'Chandi says…' He was certain that Maria would eventually grow out of it.) 'Dogs suffer from a condition called colour vision deficiency or colour blindness,' he told her. 'So, they can't tell colours apart properly.'

'Chandi,' Maria told him later. 'Shajan chachan says you have blind colourness. That's why you confuse green and orange.'

'Yeah, right!' Chandi said, giving her an ugly smile. 'As if your Shajan chachan and a bunch of idiots who call themselves doctors and scientists can decide these things. Has any dog ever gone to a scientist and told them – and it is colour blindness, not blind colourness – this? Who are you humans to make these decisions for us? For us, green is this colour, right here.' At this point, Chandi pointed to the orange Nutrine sweet. 'You humans think everything you say is right. In our world, what we say is right. Who told you that the lion was the king of animals? Did any lion come and tell you that? Or did any other animal? We don't have kings and queens and ministers and priests. You all cut down our forests and turned them into your agricultural land. And now when we walk through there, you say, oh look, animals have destroyed our crops! Did we ask you to plant your crops in our homes? If you keep taking our land, where are we supposed to go? Fed up with you lot we are, I tell you. Just you watch, one day all the animals in the forests and homes and zoos will come together and get rid of the whole lot of you from this earth!'

Chandippatti glared at Maria and ran away. Maria felt like crying. That night, in her dreams, Chandi chased her all over the place until, finally, she woke up screaming.

# 13
# Maria Decides to Grow Up

That night, when Geevarghese returned to Kottarathil Veedu with Maria, Neena was waiting for him. A friend of hers was getting married, and she wanted some money to buy a new outfit for the occasion. Usually, such requests were made to Kuncheriya, but he was away at his daughter's, having had one of his regular fallings-out with Geevarghese, so Neena had no other option than to ask her father. After listening to her, Geevarghese walked calmly to the kitchen and came back with the knife used to chop vegetables.

'Has your father stashed away money in this house?' he shouted and lunged towards Neena with the knife. Neena, who had good reflexes, moved deftly away, and took off running. Perhaps because she didn't want her entire neighbourhood to know, or perhaps because she was scared of snakes and other creepy-crawlies, Neena decided to run around the house rather than out into the street. Geevarghese chased her. Although it took them a while to figure out what in God's name was going on, Mariyamma and Sheena followed the chaser.

'Maria, tell your appachan to stop,' Mariyamma said. 'He'll kill her otherwise!'

'Serves Neenanty right,' said Maria. 'Let him. I don't care.'

Mariyamma had already taken off after Geevarghese, so she didn't hear all of what Maria said. Chandippatti was sitting around bored out of his mind, so he too took off after the runner and the chasers. Soon, as the pounding footsteps came closer, Maria realized that round one was almost complete. Neena appeared from a corner and disappeared around the other at a speed no one would have thought possible. Chandippatti followed, having overtaken everyone else who was running after Neena. When he saw Maria, he stopped to giggle at her, but Maria urged him on: 'Run, Chandi, run! Overtake everyone!' Then came Geevarghese. In his rage, he did not see Maria. Luckily, Neena was able to maintain a good lead. Sheena followed, right on Geevarghese's heels, but she did not dare stop her father.

Soon, Mariyamma came into sight, trailing far behind everyone else. Chandippatti was right behind her. This time, having overtaken everyone else, he stopped to do a little victory dance, but seeing Neena come round the corner, he took off again. Mariyamma, now at the front, or at the very back, moved to the side to allow the other runners to go past her. By now, she was not running but walking. Neena was panting heavily but maintained her speed and her lead. Then Geevarghese came round the corner.

'Appacha, enough!' Maria called out to him. 'Stop the game. It's not fun any more.'

Running at full speed, Geevarghese could not stop immediately. Like seasoned sprinters, he ran forward for a while before controlling his speed and coming to a stop.

'It's only because you stopped me, child, otherwise I would have killed her,' he declared and went inside the house.

Calling out to Geevarghese Sahada, Mariyamma sat down in the veranda and tried to catch her breath. Sheena squatted in the yard and panted until it occurred to her that it was not a position appropriate for someone of her stature, a college teacher. So, she got up and took herself inside. Unaware that Geevarghese had stopped chasing her, Neena came running around the corner. The moment she saw her, Mariyamma screamed in a voice she had never produced in her entire life: 'Stop! Get inside the house, right now!'

When the dust settled, Thomachan came out. 'What the hell is going on here?' he asked no one in particular.

After this incident, the enmity between Maria and Neena reached its peak. Finally, Neena went to Maria's parents' house and told her papa all about what was going on in Kottarathil Veedu – that Maria was always at the toddy shop with her appachan, that they did not often come home in the night ... Something else happened soon that made matters worse. One night, Maria lay down on a culvert with Geevarghese who was almost unconscious from the toddy he had drunk. She fell asleep, rolled off the culvert and cut open her head and had to be taken to the hospital.

That decided her fate. Maria was to be returned to her parents.

Hearing about the decision, Maria made a decision of her own – that it was time to grow up.

# 14

# Maria Is Given Back

Yes, that's true. When I heard of the decision, I decided to grow up. I guess this process, 'growth', may have started before I took this decision. In any case, I was sure that things would never go back to how they were.

There was nothing special or ceremonial to mark this 'giving back'. Ammachi packed an airbag with the five or six sets of clothes I had, my Bata sandals, and my A for Apple and B for Ball knickers (I was wearing the C for Cat pair). At first, I thought of leaving behind my Binaca animals, worried that Anne, Mathew and Elizabeth (I knew I had to practise calling her Lisa from then on – that's what people close to her called her) might take them. Then I realized that they would come in handy if I needed to bribe them for anything. To be honest, whenever I thought of the three of them, I felt terrified. The game was in their court now. The hidden ball, the torn frock, the broken balloons, the countless slaps, scratches and bites … they – Anne, Mathew and Lisa – would be waiting for the opportunity to take revenge.

All that week, Appachan was in a lousy mood. I spent those days gorging on the snacks Ammachi made. I was only a child, but I knew that Ammachi's home-cooked food was soon going to be a nostalgic memory for me. Appachan and I didn't go out that week, except for a single trip to the toddy shop to say goodbye to everyone. Watching Kelan's and Velayudhan's sorrow, I began to cry, which set them going, and soon we were all crying together. On the way back, I ran into Kuttappayi. Usually, I became tongue-tied before him, but on that day, I told him, with tears running down my cheeks: 'They are giving me back to my mama and papa. I'm going to be living with them from now on...' I was never sure what to call him, so I didn't call him anything. Kuttappayi said nothing. Just stood there staring at me with his pumpkin eyes. Frustrated, I repeated: 'I'm going away ... I won't come back.'

'What's it to me, girl, if you go away?' he said finally.

The failure of my first love spread across my chest like an ache. 'Give me back my Parry's and Nutrine sweets, then!' I screamed.

Another important incident that happened in that week is the disappearance of Chandippatti. It might seem overly dramatic, but that is what happened. Chandi must have gone away, convinced that life in Kottarathil Veedu without me would be boring. Ammachi said he must have gone sniffing after some new bitch. In any case, no one was in the mood to discuss his disappearance. Ammachi kept making more and more snacks as though to drown her sadness.

And what about Appachan?

Appachan barely spoke. This almost-silence would become his constant mood for the rest of his life. Appachan and Ammachi began to say, as if to console themselves, that since I was just a child, this sending away would not affect me too much. I did not try to correct them, to explain to them that it was not so. Like I said, I had already begun the process of growing up. It must be then that my belief that everything was already decided for us began to take root.

Sheenanty gave me, as though it was a going-away present, two sets of frocks and a book titled *Oru kudayum kunjupengalum*. What a silly title, I thought – 'An umbrella and a little sister' – and at first decided not to read the book. But then I changed my mind. I was curious to know why anyone would give such a stupid title to a book. Besides, it would distract me from my sadness, I thought. But that book! It was an ocean of sorrow! The moment I began reading it, all the sadness that I had locked up inside me came rushing out. I was convinced that the only reason children were born was to suffer sorrow, and that there was a huge difference between the sorrows of children and those of adults.

That week was also one of intense training. To walk wearing slippers, to eat at the dining table, to cut nails neatly, to eat only after brushing teeth, to shit only in the toilet … Ammachi and Sheenanty tried their best to teach me all these things.

'Well, you'll learn once you get there,' said Ammachi finally, frustrated. 'There's nothing you won't learn when Anna takes out her cane…'

I began to pray fervently to Geevarghese Sahada that Anna would die before I got there.

Kuncheriya valyappachan and Anna valyamma, in the brief moments when her mind was clear, were also upset that I was going away. For them, I was more of a habit than a person. Thomachan chachan even gave me a gift – a school bag. More than the gift itself, what touched me was the effort he made to get it. You will remember, he is the type of person who doesn't like to make an effort even for the most important things. And yet, he went all the way into town to buy that bag for me. I did not want to know what Neenanty felt. Nor did I have the time to find out – I was too busy gathering up my memories.

That last week was like a boundary between reality and dream. I began to think quite seriously about dying, even ate half a sheet of paper in a bid to die. But when I woke up normally the next morning, I realized that half a sheet was not enough paper to kill oneself with. So, I spent a whole hour pouring mug after mug of water over my head, hoping to catch a fever and die. I also considered running away, and only gave up on that idea when I remembered the beggar-mafia people who caught hold of children, put their eyes out and made them beg.

Ammachi used every spare moment to advise me. 'They are your parents, Maria,' she reminded me. 'You must listen to them. Anne, Mathew and Lisa are your siblings. You must love them. And it's time to stop wandering around. Good girls from good families should be at home, not roam around markets and toddy shops. And your stubbornness … it's not a good thing. When you are in other people's houses, you shouldn't behave as you please. Don't ask for things. If they give you anything, accept it respectfully. And another thing … You must stop telling lies because you'll go to hell if you lie. You must fear God and that will lead you to heaven.'

And, finally, it was Sunday. Mathew and Lisa and their papa and mama arrived. Anne wasn't with them. I tried to give Mathew and Lisa friendly smiles. As soon as they came in, their papa began to hurry everyone along. He was the type who didn't believe in wasting time unnecessarily. Their mama, meanwhile, was busy packing up all the snacks Ammachi had prepared. She was the type who never paid attention to anyone. Mathew and Lisa kept looking at me with a weird expression on their faces.

'Why is this creature coming to live with us?' they seemed to think. 'Three children are quite enough in a house. Why do we need a fourth one? That too, a devilish one like this! Come along, we'll show you!'

I went and lay down next to Appachan, pretending to be asleep. After a while, I imagined that I was dead. Finally, when I heard Ammachi calling 'Maria…' I roused myself from the world of the dead. Appachan, too, got up with me. No one embraced me or gave me kisses, perhaps because they were unsure how I would react. Holding back my tears then must have been one of the most difficult things I have ever done in my life. I did not know then that life was a series of moments when one held back one's tears.

Their mama went and sat in the front seat of the car with their papa. Those children followed, squeezing themselves into the front seat with their parents, leaving me and my airbag forlorn in the back seat. We began our journey. I vowed that I would love my parents and my siblings, prepared my mind to put up with anything and everything that came my way.

Steeped in sorrow, I fell asleep, and everything returned to normal – the same Kottarathil Veedu, the same Appachan, Ammachi, even Neenanty! But their mama roused me from my dreams, and I looked at her wondering where she had come from. Then I saw their papa, Mathew and Lisa, and that brought me back to reality. Their mama was holding out an ice cream towards me. It made me happy and I took it to be a positive sign that they had welcomed me into their family.

When we reached their home, all of them got out of the car and went inside. Their servant came and picked up my bag and she, too, went inside. I was left outside, alone. After a while, even though no one had invited me, I walked in. After all, this was supposed to me my home too from now on. I sat in a corner, trying not to attract anyone's attention, not knowing what I was supposed to do. I could hear children playing, and occasionally people came and went, but no one saw me sitting there in the corner. Soon, I began to feel hungry. I could hear noises in the kitchen – their mama was preparing something. Finally, I heard her call: 'Anne … Mathew … Lisa…' And then, after a short interval, 'Maria…' A little late, but no matter, I was happy that she called me too.

Although I was called last, I was the one to reach the dining room first. In Mama and Papa's house, it was tea. In Appachan and Ammachi's house, there was no teatime, only coffee time. The snacks – achappam, kuzhalappam and neyyappam that Ammachi had made – were set out on the table along with the tea. I did not reach for them, and only had the tea. When Mama held out a neyyappam to me, I said, 'No, thank you.' 'Nyo thyankyu,' said Mathew, imitating me, and everyone laughed. The children repeated 'nyo thyankyu' to each other in sing-song voices and made fun of me. (That Sheenanty! She was the one who taught me to say 'no, thank you'. How was I to know that you didn't say such things in your own house!) Papa was not at the table. I would learn later that his was mostly an invisible presence.

After tea, we went to have our baths. The children continued making fun of me. Lisa was the worst! When I could not take one more 'nyo thyankyu', I gave her a whack. The three of them set upon me and beat me to a corner. After the bath, Mama brought me an old frock that belonged to Anne, and when I put it on,

Anne kept saying that it was one that she had thrown away. I said I had plenty of frocks in my bag, and she said they were all crappy old things. 'Your frock is crappy,' I said before I remembered to hold my tongue, and Anne pushed me down, gave me a kick and went away.

The meal habits in the new house were very different from those at Kottarathil Veedu. There, we ate whatever we wanted whenever we wanted, sitting wherever we wanted. And because of that, in Kottarathil Veedu, someone was always eating something. But here, everyone sat around the oval dining table at designated mealtimes at regular intervals. There was fried fish, fish koottan, beef pickle and achinga ularthiyathu for dinner. The achinga cooked in coconut oil was one of my favourite things to eat, but unlike Ammachi's preparation, Mama's achinga had no taste. So, all I ate was a bit of rice with some of the beef pickle which Ammachi had made. No one asked me to eat more like they did in Kottarathil Veedu.

After dinner, Mama took me to a small room which was to be my bedroom. For the first time in my life, I was going to spend the night alone. I was terrified! But when she asked me if I was scared, I told her, in a voice trembling with fear, 'Ey, not at all.' When Mama left the room, I pulled the bedsheet over me and sobbed myself to sleep. Ghosts ... crazies ... serpents ... child-catchers ... there was nothing that didn't come that night to terrify me. And when I woke up in the morning, for the first time since I could remember, I had peed in my bed.

I began to go to school along with Anne, Mathew and Lisa. 'She's an orphan my papa adopted,' I heard Anne tell her friends in the school van. I ignored the orphan part of the story but believed the adoption part. In those early days, I believed firmly that I had been sent to this house due to some confusion that small children could not understand, and that I would be back in Kottarathil Veedu as soon as it was cleared up.

It did not take me long to understand that the family circle at the new house was complete and fully functional without me. No matter how much I tried, I could not enter that circle. If I tried and breached the circle for a moment, I was immediately thrown out with only a few scratches to show for it. As time passed, I realized the meaninglessness of it all and gave up trying to fit in. In my later life, all I would ever feel towards home and towards family relationships was a sense of detachment. Ammachi was wrong – my place was not inside the home but outside of it. But she was right too – the fault lay with me, not with my home or my family.

Discipline – that was the single most important thing in that house. (I would later come to understand the importance given to discipline in all households with small children.) I used to wonder whether it was our papa who had invented the clock.

In this new house, all the snacks were stored in big glass jars. Laddu, jalebi, cakes and other mouth-watering items smiled at me from these jars. In Kottarathil Veedu, snacks were stored in steel jars. A better system, as far as I was concerned, because they did not display themselves and tempt little children. Try as I might, I found it hard to stop loitering in front of the glass jars, ogling at their contents. But Ammachi had impressed upon me that I should not ask for anything when I go to other people's houses. So, I refrained, no matter how tempted I was. Sometimes, Mama would see me and ask: 'Do you want anything?' If my dignity was stronger than my temptation, I would answer no, but when the desire to eat those snacks got the better of my self-esteem, I would say yes, and immediately feel as though I would die of shame. Sometimes, Mama was in a good mood and would open the jars and give me something without asking whether I wanted a snack or not. Whenever she gave me two laddus or cakes, I gave one back and tried to scrape back some of my dignity. The other children opened the jars and ate what they wanted, when they wanted, and threw away what they did not finish. After all, the house was theirs, so were the cakes and laddus and jalebis. I picked up what they threw away, dusted off the less mangled pieces and ate them, always making sure that no one saw what I was doing. It was then that I resolved never to store snacks in glass jars when I would have my own house. Unfortunately, I never had a chance to put my resolution into practice because I have never had a home of my own.

I did not know then that the little mistakes we make at an age when we don't know any better have such significant impacts on the rest of our lives. If I'd known, I would have tried my best not to make them. All I can say is that I am amazed that Mama looked after me more or less even after I told her to her face how much I hated her.

Anne tortured me physically whenever she could get away with it, but it was Lisa who made my life miserable. Her torture was psychological and so much more hurtful. The moment Mama's back was turned after serving us food, Lisa grabbed the fried fish and mutta porichathu – the best of all the dishes, usually – off my plate, or the snacks at teatime. Once I complained to Mama, and the three of them objected, putting up a united front. 'Maria ate hers, we saw her!' 'If you want more, all you have to do is ask Mama. Why tell lies!' Anne added for good measure. I stopped complaining after that. The funny thing was that Lisa snatched my portion not because she wanted to eat it but because she wanted to hurt me. She managed to get me thrashed regularly by Mama as well as our teachers by other means too, such as tearing my books, scribbling in my notebooks and so on.

Of course, I did not take it all lying down; I gave as good as I got as often as I could. The difficulty was the 1:3 ratio I found myself in – me against the three of them. They could easily convince Mama and Papa that I was the one who started it. So, my retaliations had little effect.

Thankfully, though, not soon after, Mathew seemed to change. Perhaps he was bored with the childish games, he stopped torturing me, often took my side, and began to share snacks from the glass jars with me. I remember the first time he took some laddus out of the jar and gave them to me ... I refused to accept them because my enmity towards him had not ended and also because I was not willing to forgo my dignity, but that night when I was alone, I cried my heart out. That was the first time I became aware that some tears were pleasurable. After that, I began to look at him with eyes wet with gratitude. Years would pass and my enmity with Anne would also end. But Lisa ... I still have no relationship with Lisa.

It didn't take long before I became an ordinary, occasional visitor as far as Kottarathil Veedu was concerned. A significant incident during this time was Sheenanty and Jomon chachan's wedding. The night before the wedding, we children were playing, horsing around. I was fully aware of the repercussions when I decided to kill Lisa. They didn't worry me; all I wanted was for her to die. After playing, a tired Lisa sat on the concrete balustrade of the veranda upstairs with her legs dangling. I sneaked up behind her and gave her a push. My hope was that she would fall on the concrete floor of the yard below, break her head open and die. But the horrible girl landed in the grass verge and lay there, bleeding and wailing at the top of her voice. As the adults ran to her, I retained the small hope that she might yet die.

What followed was a festival of thrashing … Mama, Papa, Ammachi, Neenanty – I was beaten by everyone. Even Anne insinuated herself into the melee and gave me a slap or two. It was only after I was beaten thoroughly that they took Lisa to the hospital. Tears flowed down my cheeks, but I wasn't crying. Having expected a more serious outcome, I was sad that she didn't die. The only consolation was the demon girl had broken her leg and was held up for about two months.

Everyone hated me in those moments, even Appachan, Ammachi, Sheenanty and Thomachan chachan, so I don't have to tell you about Papa, Mama, Anne and Mathew. I, too, was overcome with hatred – hatred for the whole world. I kept shouting that I had tried to kill Lisa and that I would do so again if I had another opportunity. 'I will kill you too,' I screamed at Anne. 'Enough!' Sheenanty shouted, finally. 'I won't let you spoil my wedding like this.' And with that, she grabbed me and dragged me off to her room.

As soon as the wedding was over, they took me to a psychiatrist. Now that I am a veteran of the system, I am amazed that they thought a psychiatrist's help was required for such insignificant things. This psychiatrist, he looked funny with his dyed hair and Bulganin beard. The skin on his chin was stained with the black dye he had used. When he spoke, he stressed some letters and syllables unnecessarily – 'ttrreetment' and 'ssaikkhology' and 'perrrforrrm' – and had a particular fondness for the word 'circumstance'. He sat me down and schooled me on good behaviour, even gave me a book about a girl who was well behaved. The story was, well, let's just say so utterly unbelievable given how well behaved this girl was. And in order to impress the readers with her good behaviour, she put herself through all kinds of unnecessary dangers and adversities. Anyway, I didn't really understand even half of what the psychiatrist told me, so I agreed to everything. What I did understand was:

I must read that book.

I must strive to be a good girl like the girl in that book.

I agreed to everything then because I hadn't read the book yet, and when I did read it, I found it utterly boring. When it was time to leave, I told the psychiatrist, very casually, about the dye stains on his face. My intentions were good, I wasn't making fun of him. There was nothing to make fun of about a few black stains on the face anyway. But it embarrassed him, and my papa and mama. This is the problem with adults – they take everything way too seriously and make problems out of them.

Things didn't improve much even after the visit to the psychiatrist. The enmity between Lisa and me increased in intensity. Now she had justifications for whatever she wanted to do to me – I was, after all, her future killer. The attempted murder had made me bolder too, and so I retaliated openly and hard. 'O Lord, please let me not run into her tomorrow,' we both prayed to Karthav Eesho Mishiha as only children can do.

In the midst of all this, one fine day, Anna valyamma died. I think even the dementia got bored with her. Appachan always said that the dementia had targeted her even when she was young, that she was born with a tendency towards dementia. And he always used the word 'tendency' in English. As he grew older, Appachan developed a tendency to use English words willy-nilly. Remember that he never studied beyond Class 4. This was a tendency cultivated by television. For instance, everyone was beginning to feel that Appachan would die soon. So, the other day, I began bawling loudly, demanding that he not die. Suddenly, what do you know, Appachan says, 'Maria, don't make things difficult for me,' in proper English!

When she was sure that it was time for her die, Anna valyamma said her goodbyes, turned over in her bed to face west, and lay there. No one was bothered because they all thought it was the dementia acting out, and so it was a while before anyone noticed that she was dead. Poor Anna valyamma … The truth is that no one cared much about her in life or in death. She had always been proud to declare that she was a member of the Kottarathil Veedu family. Appachan had her buried in the family grave.

After I was sent away, I began to talk less and less until I became silent enough for people to think I could not speak. It was a habit I cultivated in order to avoid attracting people's attention. I spoke in the night, in the privacy of my little room, to Appachan, Chandippatti, Karthav Eesho Mishiha and anyone else I wanted. I spoke to them to my heart's content.

As for school…

It is better not to talk about school. When I was little, I used to wonder whether all the teachers with their sturdy canes were just waiting for me to appear. The children at my school were very creative and gave nicknames to all the teachers. Crazy Chacko, Prancing Kunjamma, Black Omana, White Omana, Suppose Saramma…

Crazy Chacko was my maths teacher in Class 5. Once, I had a doubt about a maths problem and asked him a question. He punished me by making me write 'I will not ask questions in class' one hundred times in my imposition notebook. True story, I swear to you! Still, this type of punishment was nothing compared to the beating meted out by Kidukkan Kanaran. And this beating became entirely insignificant when Pathrose the Bald came up behind you and rubbed himself against you under the pretext of checking your classwork. All life's miseries are relative in intensity.

Every time someone talks nostalgically about their childhood, I am convinced that they are lying. The colourfulness of childhood … the joyous wonder … the innocence… Bullshit! I am yet to meet a child who personifies innocence. And as for me, I don't remember many feelings other than fear and hatred. I guess my childhood wonderments died under the cloud that was the constant expectation of punishment.

There was one summer vacation when I went back to Kottarathil Veedu and spent a month there. They were amazed by this new, mature Maria. All except Appachan, who did not like this grown-up Maria. There was something weird between us, I could see, a discomfort. I thought his love for me had dissipated, that Appachan thought he didn't have to love me any more because I was no longer a member of Kottarathil Veedu.

At night, I told Ammachi that I liked to sleep alone, and she looked at me as though I had said something really sad. She sat beside me and asked me all about my life with my family. Everything is fine, I reassured her. In the morning when I woke up, I found her sleeping next to me.

Life in Kottarathil Veedu went on even though so many people had left – me, Sheenanty, Thomachan chachan, Anna valyamma … One day, Appachan and I were having our coffee at the dining table. Kuncheriya valyappachan was at the last stage of his breakfast, eating the boiled ethappazham. Suddenly, he gave a surprised laugh and began nodding, the half-chewed piece of banana still in his mouth.

'Looks like Anna valyamma's dementia has caught hold of Appan,' Appachan whispered in my ear.

'Valyappacha, what's up? Why are you laughing?' I asked.

'The thing is, child, all this time I have been trying to remember something I had forgotten a long time ago,' Kuncheriya valyappachan said. 'And it has come to me suddenly. It's funny that I've been struggling to remember such a small little thing!'

'What is it?' Appachan could not hold back his curiosity.

'It's about Anna. I wanted to get her married off. And then I forgot all about it! That's what I was trying to remember all these years.'

'Good thing you remembered it now, she'll be happy in her grave,' said Appachan. 'What a thing to forget!'

'It wasn't on purpose! I just forgot. Would I have tried so hard to remember all these years if I had allowed it to slip my mind on purpose? To be honest, it is Shoshamma who's to blame. It was she who dissuaded me, saying that where else would poor, orphan Anna find a home as secure as this.'

Kuncheriya valyappachan concluded his story and went back to eating his banana with the surprised smile still on his face.

Appachan and I went to the pond to catch some fish. There were fewer fish in the pond, Appachan declared, because no one was there to catch them. It was Appachan's discovery that if people fished regularly at a pond, the fish living there would reproduce faster and in larger numbers, afraid that otherwise they would become extinct. If not, they'd think they had all the time in the world and chill out and become lazy. Anyway, even after a couple of hours of fishing, we managed to catch barely anything, and the tilopi we did catch continued staring at us even after they were dead, with eyes full of surprise, fear and accusations. We took the fish to Ammachi, but when we sat down for lunch, there was no tilopi curry. Ammachi said that even after they became curry, the fish kept looking at her with their little eyes full of fear, so she threw it away. A whole potful of terrified-fish curry!

By the time I came back to Kottarathil Veedu for another holiday, it had become almost empty. Sheenanty and Thomachan chachan had already left, and now Neenanty had also married and gone away to live in her husband's house. Eetha had become very old and gone back to her own house to await death, handing the kitchen over to her daughter, Molly. Ittan, our karyasthan who took care of all the affairs of the house, barely came to work because there was nothing much to take care of any more.

Kuncheriya valyappachan spent most of his time in bed, his trusted Bible held close to his chest. He was in a terrible state. His death was not imminent – it would be another five years before he would die – but he feared dying more than death itself. He believed it was unfair that his mother and his wife, who were sure to go to hell, had died peacefully. At the same time, he understood that having such thoughts constituted defiance of God, which increased his terror. And when he realized that such thoughts might interfere with his entry into heaven, he began to think about suicide. But suicide was a most heinous wrong in the eyes of God.

Towards the end of his life, Kuncheriya valyappachan became stubborn like a little child. He demanded that Ammachi remain by his side at all times, and expected her to reassure him, again and again, that he would go to heaven. On that visit, I barely even saw Ammachi. She was always in his room, and I was terrified of going anywhere near him because when I went to him, I thought he exuded a deep hatred for me. I would later realize that this hatred was not aimed specifically at me. By the end of his life, he displayed such a hatred for everyone and everything that was alive, that was still endowed with life force.

By the time he was a hundred years old, Kuncheriya valyappachan had begun to decay. Many a time, he reached death's door but fought his way back to life, powered by his intense fear of dying and abiding love for life and for food. Finally, when there was no more fight left in his body or mind, he accepted the final sacraments for his soul and prepared himself for entering the heavenly abode. And yet, as the time of his death approached, his face contorted in terror. Forget about children, even adults were reluctant to kiss his face for a final time after he was dead.

It was around this time that we acquired a television set. It would have a lasting impact on my life. I was in search of someone I could feel close to in those days, and the TV brought me Boris Becker. I swore lasting allegiance to him. But it was difficult to keep this promise because, pretty soon, he began losing all his games. It was Becker who lost but it was Karthav Eesho Mishiha who bore the brunt of my anger and sorrow at his failure. The fact that the electricity would cut off every now and then during the course of a match also soured my relationship with Karthav. Every time this happened, I would run to my room, kneel in front of the small picture of Jesus stuck to the wall, and pray earnestly. But, overcome with my intense love for Becker, I would lose my patience within five minutes. In my reckoning, five seconds were plenty to bring back the electricity, and here I was, generously allowing five whole minutes, taking into consideration the dire state of electricity distribution in our country. Besides, bringing the power back was not such a miraculous task. For someone like me who believed in miracles such as water turning into wine and the raising of Lazarus, reconnecting electricity was only a dookly thing. Still, many times it remained cut off until the game was over, and as though to rub salt on sores, it came back just as Becker left the court. Either Karthav did not like tennis, or He did not like Boris Becker. Or, most likely, He did not like me! It could also be that even Karthav found His powers limited when it came to the aforementioned state of the electricity distribution system in our land. I feel bad now when I think about Karthav waiting for the arrival of our lineman Babu, bathed in the abuse showered by a little girl…

My papa came to know of my intense love for Boris Becker. He knew nothing at all about sports in general or tennis in particular, or about the star. And yet he exclaimed: 'What is she jumping up and down about him for? Look at his eyebrows … like white cockroaches!'

The other important thing that happened around this time was that I became a communist. A thirteen-year-old communist. A God-fearing communist like every other communist in the land.

It happened unexpectedly.

Reading Maxim Gorky's *Mother* was the main inspiration. It was to mark a turning point in my life. I began to think that I was born to be a communist. Then I read C. Radhakrishnan's *Munpe Parakkunna Pakshikal* and signed the book with my own blood! I didn't cut myself specifically for this purpose – I just used the blood that oozed out when I accidentally nicked myself while cutting my fingernails. Why waste it, I thought. I think I would have been a communist guerrilla if I'd lived closer to the Bolivian forests. I couldn't tell you why, but I didn't find the forests around us particularly romantic.

If someone were to ask me what the most difficult period in my life was, even if I lived to be a hundred years old, I would answer: childhood. It was the single most torturous period I endured.

Lisa … Anne … Papa … Mama…

The snacks in the glass jars.

Maths, physics, chemistry, and the endless confounding equations.

Boris Becker who continued to lose all his matches.

Karthav Eesho Mishiha.

All the sins I committed in full view of Karthav.

My continued stealing (mostly from my own home).

Disrespecting my parents and teachers.

Telling Mama to her face that I hated her.

Fighting with my siblings.

Praying that Anne and Lisa would die.

Constantly killing centipedes, lizards and cockroaches.

Trying to kill Lisa.

Talking during the Holy Qurbana … dozing off (which constituted the additional sin of enraging our parish priest, Father Jacob).

Not reading the Bible regularly (and leaving out sections when I did read it).

Because of all this, along with my parents, Sunday school teachers and the parish priest, I too was convinced that I was headed straight for hell. In those days, I was a believer. I had learned to believe without questioning.

For a long while after, Appachan and Kottarathil Veedu were absent from my life. If you ask me what was in my life in that period, I don't remember. Like Aravind says, I floated through life. Until, one day years later, vomiting out all the bread I had eaten thus far in my life, I went to Kottarathil Veedu with the sole purpose of eating Ammachi's appam and chicken curry.

Appachan was in the easy chair on the veranda waiting for me ... He had been sitting there for years.

# 15

# Maria's Return

Years later, Maria came looking for me.

In actual fact, Maria didn't come looking for me, but I like to think that is why she came back. She looked as though she had walked out of a dream. At first, she didn't seem to notice me sitting on the veranda in my easy chair. Then she glanced at me, said, 'Ah, Appachan,' and went inside. My heart ached like it was about to burst. Then I thought, this is Maria after all, anything is possible, and followed her into the kitchen where Mariyamma was cleaning rice. In the shock of seeing Maria unexpectedly after all these years, the winnow in Mariyamma's hand fell to the floor, scattering rice everywhere. I began laughing. And I was so certain that Maria would laugh with me, but she just looked at me as though wondering what was so funny about a fallen winnow and a handful of scattered rice. I didn't know what to do, and as I stood there confused, she turned to Mariyamma.

'Ammachi, I want something to eat,' she said, as though years hadn't passed since she had last seen us.

Mariyamma, still shocked, served up some appam and chicken curry. Maria polished off a dozen appams and a couple of plates of the chicken, and went off to sleep. When she woke up and came out, she was laughing.

'I thought I'd die laughing when I saw you drop the winnow and the rice,' she said.

That only increased Mariyamma's sense of shock and confusion, but it made me happy. Because that was the Maria I knew. But I also felt sad because all these years had passed and Maria had not changed.

The last time I saw her, Maria was eighteen years old. A few days later, Anna called to tell us that she had run away. We don't know much about her life after that, and she, well, she can't remember anything. We heard she was studying and working at the same time. Maria did not do these things because she was a brave girl – in fact, she is not all that brave. I think she does these things because she can't help it. She did not attend Anne's wedding. Anna told everyone that she had some sort of exam that she could not miss, something that was important enough to decide the course of her life.

Some time later, Anna called to inform us that Maria had married someone, and then a while later, she called again, this time with the news that Maria was divorced. For the longest time after, we didn't hear anything at all about Maria. After she came back on that first visit to eat appam and chicken curry, Maria began to visit us regularly. Whenever Mariyamma asked her about her marriage or about her life, she just shrugged and said, 'I don't remember anything, Ammachi, truly.' That was one good thing about her, she forgot things quickly, and just flowed through life. I wanted to tell her that I would always be with her, no matter what. But what can I say ... By the time she came back to us, my life was almost over.

# Part III

# 16

# Thus, Too, Some Lives

'I'm Maria. But if you were to ask me, "Are you Maria?", I am not sure I could answer with certainty. My name, in any case, is Maria, and there isn't much else I can say about myself. I could tell you, "I'm so-and-so's daughter," but if our parents don't feel proud when we say it, there is not much point in making that claim, is there? It seems my papa once commented: "When we think of our children most parents feel love and tenderness, but when I think of Maria, I shiver as though I have a fever." Now, if you ask me what I do, I don't like that question either. Is it necessary that everyone should be doing something? The only interesting thing I could tell you about myself is that one of my great-grandfathers – when I say great-grandfather, he was like nine generations removed – was a super magician as well as a priest. Chirammel Kathanar, that was his name. The world-renowned magician Kadamattathu Kathanar learned magic from this ancestor of mine. Chirammel Kathanar was so much more skilled than his pupil, but for some unknown reason, he has been banished from history. I am thinking of doing some research into the circumstances that led to this complete erasure of Chirammel Kathanar.'

When Aravind returned from a long journey, a young woman, drunk off her head, was in Hari's room, and this was how she introduced herself. In the eagerness to share the story of her ancestor, she choked on the spicy snack she was chewing and rushed outside, gagging. Aravind went after her and gently patted her back as she heaved. For the first time in the thirty-five years he had been alive in this world, Aravind felt that his life had some identifiable objectives. He did not think, in that moment, whether the life objective of a fairly well-known artist like him was rubbing the back of a drunk woman. Because what was meant to happen had already happened. Aravind had fallen in love. When Aravind went after her, the woman was a stranger to him, but when he came back, he was holding his lover who was tired from throwing up. There, really, is only so much to life.

The next day when they met, Maria told Aravind: 'Hello, I am Maria.'

'I know,' Aravind said with a naughty smile that suited him well. 'The granddaughter of Chirammel Kathanar who taught magic to Kadamattathu Kathanar.'

Overcome with shyness, Maria looked at him, and Aravind was overcome with love.

'Poor thing, she is, really…' Hari said when he heard about Aravind's love for Maria. 'But don't expect to marry her and live happily ever after. Because, you know … she is not that normal.'

The last sentence was in English even though Hari was not someone who used English as a matter of course. Soft-hearted Hari used English only when he had to say something difficult or sad because, according to him, as a language, English was less emotional than Malayalam.

'Well, who among us is really normal?' Aravind asked with a sorrowful smile.

A genuine question. Was Hari, who had left the sprawling mansion of his millionaire father to live like a poor person, normal? Was Vinayakan, who spent all his time playing chess and smoking charas, both of which had affected his brain, normal? Or was Shamseer, who sat unmoving for days, declaring that he was an electrical transformer? Then there was Aravind ... Aravind was normal because he was the one who had to take care of them all. Laughter bubbled up in him, a huge, sad laughter.

All that happened a long time ago, but in their world, especially in Hari's room, time had no relevance. They were the remnants of some long-ago time, people who had been banished, or had banished themselves, from the present ... People for whom time had stopped.

And now...

Now, Maria is getting drunk with Aravind, Hari, Vinayakan, Jayan and Shamseer. Maria is not all that keen on the taste of the rough alcohol, 'kattu rum' as Hari calls it, that they are drinking. Then again, no one really drinks to enjoy the taste. It is Maria's greatest wish that she could get drunk on orange juice. And Aravind and Vinayakan have no doubt that Maria is quite capable of that. Maria likes to mix Coca-Cola with her rum. Hari and Aravind are dead against Coca-Cola given the problems the cola companies create by harvesting all the water and exploiting the land and the people. Vinayakan, meanwhile, says that the cola companies' exploitation is only a part of the inevitable destruction of everything in this world, the destruction that all living and non-living things must endure. Anyway, Maria loves rum and cola, and when she says, 'Please, please...' Aravind feels an indescribable softness in the middle of his heart and sets aside his anti-cola attitude temporarily. And Hari will look angrily at him, only to smile soon enough as he knows how things are. What chance for anti-capitalism or anti-cola standpoints when faced with love! On that day, though, having the additional problem of being broke, Maria has to drink her rum with water from the tap. When she was a child, Maria had read a lot of children's stories from the Soviet Union, and her greatest wish was to taste the oats they gave to their horses and the vodka that the grown-ups drank. And she did when she grew up but hated the taste of both. Maria did not try oats ever again, but vodka ... well, no one drinks vodka for its taste. Vinayakan is convinced that there is an international conspiracy behind the transformation of the oats that the white man's horses ate into the main food of the Malayali. Vinayakan is able to see into things in ways that ordinary people cannot. For example, this, right now:

Maria is picking up the bits of mixture that had fallen on the floor and eating them. She is not doing it because she is drunk; she feels genuine happiness in picking things off the floor and eating them. Aravind scolds her, but Vinayakan disagrees.

'You should be supporting her,' he says, 'because eating things off the floor increases our immunity.'

Maria looks up and rewards everyone, especially Vinayakan, with a sparkling smile.

'Don't know what it is, but I love eating off the floor,' she says.

'Ideally, even when our food is on the plate, we should take it and rub it around on the floor for a bit before eating,' says Vinayakan. 'It is important that we maximize our immunity in this polluted world.'

'Aiyo! That's a bit too much for me,' Maria says apologetically, as though owning up to some shortcoming.

Vinayakan always spoke in formal language, reminding Maria of her social studies classes at school, and of Prithviraj Chauhan, Chetak, Muhammad bin Tughlaq and his governmental reforms…

'So many people were involved in so many governmental reforms…'

'What did you say?' Aravind asks.

'Oh, nothing,' says Maria. 'I was just remembering something.'

Shamseer does not take part in any of these discussions. Because Shamseer is a transformer and transformers do not speak. Still, this transformer drinks alcohol and smokes ganja. Shamseer transforms into a transformer only every now and then. When he is not a transformer, he is a happy, jolly man. And he wrote poetry in both states, but only the poems written when he was a transformer were accepted for publication. The others came back with a 'we regret…' note from the editor.

Now, suddenly, the transformer speaks to Aravind. 'Why don't you paint something like *The Potato Eaters* and call it *Kanjikudiyanmaar?*'

Ordinarily, he does not speak when he is a transformer, but Shamseer is a great Van Gogh fan, and the urge to see a painting in his style that depicted the people of our land as 'kanji eaters' might have been too much to bear. Aravind smiles and says, 'Let me see,' and Maria feels like kissing him because Aravind never says 'no' or 'can't' to anyone. Poor Aravind. Maria reaches up and kisses him on his cheek, and Aravind brushes his lips against hers as though he is extending her kiss. Maria knows Aravind will never paint that picture. Aravind's favourite artist is Chagall, and

Maria's is Bruegel. She could spend hours looking at his *Two Chained Monkeys* or *The Wedding Dance* with all the men with their 'shoo' poking out of their breeches. Aravind was the one who introduced all these artists to Maria, and now Bruegel and Goya are like Mathiri valyammachi and Kuncheriya valyappachan to her.

Hari sets out for the wine shop to get more booze. Wine shops and bars are like his own home for him. Hari's story is funny. He is the only son of a multi-millionaire businessman, but he left home, ridden with the guilt of living such a privileged life in this world full of starving people. Aravind, Vinayakan and Shamseer call him 'Modern Buddhan' affectionately. Maria knows that if she had been in his place, she would not have done such a thing. So much money! Imagine how much biriyani one could eat with all that money! Maria relates everything to do with money to biriyani. But Hari doesn't want to eat biriyani – or anything else for that matter. All he wants is plenty of booze – doesn't matter if it is Tusker or Jawan or the local brew – and drugs. Maria has asked him several times why he couldn't do that from the soft-as-snow bed in his mansion. And every time, his answer has been the same: 'You won't understand.'

Jayan is, in the language of the newspapers, a public-minded lawyer. So many people come to him for so many things, and Jayan always says to them, 'Don't worry about it, we've got someone who can sort it out.' There is nowhere on earth where Jayan doesn't have 'someone'. 'He has someone even in the White House,' Hari says, making fun of him. Unlike Hari, Vinayakan and Shamseer, Jayan is not always drowning in alcohol. He only drinks to feel refreshed in the middle of his various responsibilities.

And there are others too, who come and go in that room to drink, to take drugs. Even a rich person becomes poor upon entering that room. It has a look of penury, and is only as big as a toilet in Hari's father's mansion, but it makes space for so many people to sleep. Aravind calls it the world's only real socialist state. And that is the honest truth. There have been times when up to ten people brushed their teeth with the only toothbrush in the room. Vinayakan does not have a toothbrush because he does not brush his teeth or wash. Watching Hari brush his teeth after a long night of boozing, Vinayakan will look at him uncomprehendingly and ask, 'Why, thayoli, why brush your teeth when you're only going to pour kattu rum down your throat again?' Vinayakan never calls Hari by his name, and given that he has no attachment with his father or mother, Hari feels thayoli – 'motherfucker' – is his real name. Vinayakan cannot understand why one needs to brush teeth and shower and so on only to get drunk and high. Not that Hari understands it either; it is just a habit. Vinayakan and Hari are very fond of each other. Aravind and Maria are very fond of each other. All four of them like each other very much, and all four of them like Jayan and Shamseer a little less. Maria does not know why this is so, and perhaps neither do the rest of them. Even though they like each other very much, Hari and Vinayakan quarrel all the time. And when they do, Vinayakan banishes Hari from Hari's room, like Geevarghese used to banish Kuncheriya from his own home. Then Hari goes to Aravind's to spend the night. Sometimes, Vinayakan and Hari do not go out of the room for months – going to the wine shop or to score drugs is not 'going out' for them. The tiny shop next door sells drugs, but Vinayakan travels kilometres to buy drugs from a woman named Sarasu. The reason is that Sarasu pulls out the drugs she sells from inside her blouse. When asked whether the drugs are more intoxicating if they come out of her blouse,

Vinayakan says, 'Intoxication is a state of mind,' and Maria is reminded again of Tughlaq's governmental reforms.

All Maria remembers from the fifteen years of her school life are ten or fifteen things:

> HCF, LCM, sin theta, cos theta, right-angled triangle, set square.
> Tughlaq's governmental reforms, Bajirao Peshwa, Chetak.
> Cross-section of the kidney.
> Take a tumbler as shown in the picture.
> Latitude, longitude, equator; $E = MC^2$.
> Nithyabhyasi aanaye edukkum.
> Carbon monoxide, lithium, helium.
> MooṬHan peeḌHathil irunnu.
> Gai ek paltu jaanvar hai.
> Chandrakkaran.
> Paraganam, Prakashasamsleshanam.
> Suppose a cobra bites a man...

That is it! As for extra-curricular activities, these are all the things she can remember:

> Devaki teacher and her cane (in the first two years).
> The new school from Class 3 onwards.
> In Class 4, feeling attracted to Ajay George from the big school next door (for the sole reason that he wore a tie).
> In Class 5, feeling attracted to Sreekumar who was a boarder (those who were in the boarding school had a certain ... something).
> Class 6 – a complete blank.

*Feeling attracted to James sir who taught English, and to Sreekumar's older brother Jayashankar who was in Class 9.*

*In Class 8, falling in love with Rony Thomas who changed schools and joined her class; feeling attracted to Savio who was in Class 7 and a boarder; and among adults, to Johnson chettan who taught Sunday School.*

*In Class 9, in love with Tisson Kurian; and among grown-ups, with Eldos chettan who was the sacristan at the church. And brushing Tisson aside, falling back in love with Rony Thomas.*

*In Class 10 ... Oh, that was proper love. Love like never before. Liju George Baby who was in 10D (Maria was in 10C) and Maria went for maths tuition to the same teacher. Liju George Baby who rode a brand-new blue BSA bicycle ... The gorgeous Liju George Baby ... One day, when, overcome with desire, Maria looked at Liju George Baby who sat opposite, what did she see but Liju George Baby gazing at her! That was when Maria understood the secrets behind what went on between men and women. What an experience that was...*

Vinayakan says that Maria should become a writer, because enough literary elucidation has been given to men's drinking but no one has really written about women's drinking. When people write about women, they only discuss their sexuality, sexual dissatisfaction to be precise. Satisfied or dissatisfied, what is there to write so much about sexuality? Besides, Maria could write about men from a female point of view. Aravind knows that is stupid because Maria does not have a male or female point of view. Maria only has a Marian point of view.

Maria does not want to write about drinking or about sexuality. Nor does she have anything else to write about it. There is only one thing she wants to write about, and it is this:

Maria is afraid of public spaces. The reason being that she was born a woman, which was, in itself, a terrible thing. But to be born a woman in this land … nothing more terrible could happen to a person. Every pig in this land thinks that a woman who steps into the public space is their property. So, every day before going out, before getting into a bus, Maria thinks long and hard and has a chat with herself:

*'Okay, so, there will be wolf whistles. Don't take it seriously. It is natural that men whistle and sing obscene songs when they see a woman, as natural as a bull raising its tail to take a shit. They can't help it. Don't take the obscene songs seriously either.*

*And they'll make comments … Don't take those seriously.*

*So, what should be taken seriously?*

*If someone gets physical, that will be serious. But, within it, what is really serious?*

*Okay, if my breasts are grabbed, that will be most serious. If my ass is grabbed that will be serious too.*

*What about other body parts?*

*Well, best to decide on the spot, depending. But breasts/ass grabbing will be taken seriously. O My Lord, I am sick and tired of having to watch over my breasts and ass…'*

In connection to this, Maria has a message for the government too:

*'The constitution of this great country that is India has given me five fundamental freedoms and several associated rights. I have only one thing to say to the sarkar. Take it back, all of it, and give me just this one thing: the right to be free from being ogled at.'*

Other than this, Maria has, despite what Vinayakan thinks, nothing to write about. Writers are foolish people who think of themselves as doing great things, as people who are above ordinary folk.

It was Hari whom Maria became acquainted with first. Maria had worked in a publishing company for a while – for a while meaning one month – and Hari had been a graphic designer in the same company. They were not all that close while working there, just a bit more than acquaintances. Hari left the company before Maria did. One day, as she sat in her office, Maria felt an intense desire to drink alcohol, but there was nowhere where women could drink in peace. In those days, Maria lived in a ladies' hostel, sharing a room with three other women. When she racked her brain (it was only for such things that Maria racked her brain), Hari's face came to her, and she rushed off to his room. It was the first time Maria was going to a man's room. Until then, she had only seen men's rooms in films, and in the films, every time a woman went to a man's room, there would be a rape. Even though she stayed in Hari's room, drinking herself senseless, Hari did not rape her. But she was expelled from the hostel because she had disappeared without informing them. So, without further ado, Maria stayed on in Hari's room. Hari and Vinayakan liked Maria very much – she was more abnormal than they were – and they would only have been happy if she continued to live with them permanently. But their room was a place where so many people came and went, friends and strangers. What if one of them raped her? It was this thought that made Hari arrange for Maria to stay with Aisha, as a paying guest in Saralachechi's house.

All of them love that spacious house – all of them meaning Aisha, Nimmi, Radhika and Maria. 'The House of Peace', Aisha says, often. Her own house is only two kilometres away, but Aisha likes this house better. Aisha's parents are activists, and constantly argue about something or the other. 'They would be truly upset if there were no problems in this land,' Aisha says. Theirs was a love marriage, but immediately after marriage, Aisha's father's activism gave way to chauvinism. 'All men are conceited bastards,' declares Aisha every now and then, 'and my father is the most conceited of them all.' Aisha is a copywriter in an advertising agency. Once, she made a poster with the caption 'All men are conceited bastards' and the picture of a pig, and asked Maria what she thought of it. Maria said the pig looked cute.

For Radhika, it is 'The House of Comfort'. Radhika's parents are, as Malathichechi, Saralachechi's cook, says, in 'Persia'. Every country outside India is Persia to Malathichechi. Since her parents sent her more than enough money, Radhika did course after course, but she only did those that took a year to finish. She completed courses in jewellery design and front office management, but left cookery, interior decoration, fashion design and vegetable carving halfway through. When she was studying vegetable carving, Radhika bought kilo after kilo of cabbage, carrot, tomato and cucumber, and used specialist knives to try and carve them into Santa Claus and butterflies and flowers. These pieces of 'abstract art' were turned into sambar and aviyal by Malathichechi. When she was studying cookery, Radhika, in a burst of excitement, even tried to get Saralachechi to let Malathichechi go, but Saralachechi was clever enough not to listen to her. Radhika would continue starting and dropping courses until she got married. Aisha says she was born to do this, but then according to Aisha, everyone is born to do something or the other.

As for Saralachechi … Saralachechi is the owner of the house, 'a poor, middle-aged widow' in her own words. She learned these types of expressions from watching the serials on TV. By 'poor' Saralachechi means 'virtuous' and 'chaste' and such. In her estimation, a human being's average lifespan must be around a hundred and thirty years. That is why she is 'middle-aged' at the age of sixty-five. The widowhood – that, in fact, is absolutely true. Her late husband, Kumaran Nair, sat on the living room wall with a sandalwood garland adorning his chest. He did not give her any children, but before he died, he had provided enough resources for her to live a good life.

Saralachechi loves sweets. In fact, she lives to eat sweets and watch serials. Once, Aisha brought her the best pastries available in the city, but Saralachechi did not like them. She prefers local sweets. Aisha says that is a matter of habit.

Then there is the worship. Saralachechi is extremely devout. Every day at five in the morning, she bathes and walks to the temple in her wet clothes. Her devotionals are notorious in the neighbourhood. She appeases the gods with her devotional songs before removing herself to the material world of TV serials.

Aisha says we should tolerate Saralachechi's little foibles given that she has been living all on her own for over thirty years. Nimmi says Saralachechi is the craziest person she has ever come across. It is important to take Nimmi's opinion somewhat seriously because she lived in America until she was thirty years old and has seen something of the world. She and her parents are American citizens. They are very keen to get her married, but Nimmi has no such thoughts. Her younger sister is married and has two children. At the time of the wedding, Nimmi's mother was more concerned about having an elephant to welcome the guests than about the prospective bridegroom. Nimmi is doing some research into sexuality although, according to Aisha, she is only researching the practical side of things. Nimmi does not like Kumaran Nair. 'That asshole is staring at me,' she screams every now and then, pointing at his photo on the living room wall.

Saralachechi opened up her home for paying guests five years ago as a way to reduce her loneliness. There were only two in the beginning, but when it began bringing a steady income, Saralachechi got more interested. Each guest paid five thousand rupees. 'That cunning lady is getting twenty thousand rupees from us! That's hilarious!' Nimmi says. Nimmi loves the word 'hilarious'.

Since Maria does not have a proper job or income, it is Aravind who pays her rent. Finding a job is difficult for Maria, but it is even more difficult to keep the job once she gets it because Maria struggles with understanding what other people say, and they find it hard to understand what Maria says.

On the teapoy in the living room is a paper with a picture of Karthav Eesho Mishiha. Maria takes it and looks at it with interest. It says:

*Listen, I stand at the door and knock. If any hear and open the door, I will come into their house and eat with them, and they will eat with me.*

Maria reads this and says: 'Listen, it's not good to have this much self-confidence when you expect someone to feed you for free out of the goodness of their heart.'

It was a few years ago when Maria was going through the nitty-gritty of divorce that Karthav Eesho Mishiha came looking for her for the first time. He had come pretending to give her expert advice, but Maria had not understood this.

'Have you forgotten me?' That was His first question. Maria thought that the question was overly dramatic. At first, she did not recognize this man with very dark skin and a dark beard.

'Odekkaara! It's you, Karthaveeshomishiha!' she said when she recognized Him. 'What brings you here?'

'Old acquaintance ... I mean, well, I thought I'd refresh our old acquaintance,' He said in a voice that had not even the semblance of self-confidence.

'But you've become so dark! The Karthav I knew had skin like rose petals!'

'Well, it's been over two thousand years...' Karthav said, and sighed deeply.

Maria noticed He was sighing constantly. 'Do your believers know that you've grown so dark?'

'Don't think so,' He sighed again.

'It's a matter of great political importance! A new leader for the marginalized all over the world! A Third World leader! That's a great idea. Have you heard of the Third World?'

'No, I haven't ... But, Maria, listen ... Actually, I've come to tell you someth—'

'No? Don't you even have the least sense of politics? Look, I am a Third World citizen. Why? Because my country has no money. All the monied ones are in the First World.'

'So, where is the Second World?'

'Oh, there's a lot you'll need to learn if you want to understand that. The Second World is not here at the moment. They were here until recently, but not any more.'

'Where did they go?'

'Shheda! You're so annoying! Well, sometime ago, there were these countries called socialist countries. They are the Second World. That doesn't matter though, because only the First and the Third Worlds are important to us. You know the difference between the haves and the have-nots – that's exactly what the First World and the Third World are about.'

'The haves and the have-nots ... That's me that said it, isn't it?'

'Yeah, well, when you said it, it was cold kanji. But when Marx said it, it became piping hot soup! Imbued with revolutionary fervour.'

'Still ... it is my saying...'

'Oh, don't bother with all that old stuff. Do you know what's wrong with us black and brown people the world over? We've never had a good leader. All we have are athletes and singers and such, and we can't win revolutions by running and singing. A black Karthav! Just watch, from tomorrow all the oppressed in the world will congregate behind you. Good thing that you came to me first. You've come to the right place!'

'But ... don't you think there's been some misunderstanding? Is it right to impose upon me, the God, the opinion of the people? It should be the other way round, no?'

'It was like that until recently, yes, but now we need a god who will listen to what we have to say. From now on, gods don't need to lead us. In fact, it is for your benefit too, because already a large section of humanity thinks that you all take the side of the rich and the powerful all the time.'

'I very much hope we can change that misunderstanding.'

'In that case, you better let us lead you. After all, this is a revolution. Everyone has to make sacrifices.'

'I ... You mean I am going to be part of a revolution?'

'Yes! Aren't you proud to be involved?'

'Meaning I will lead the revolution?'

'Don't fill your head with such foolishness. In the eyes of the world, you will be our leader, but in actual fact, you will only do what we ask you to do. Understood?'

'I guess...'

'Look here, there's the Indian president and then there's the American president. Both are presidents but they are entirely different. The American president has real power because he is the one who makes the decisions that are acted on in his name. But the Indian president is not like that. The decisions made in his name are made by other people. And yet, both are presidents.'

'Are you saying I will be like the Indian president?'

'Exactly! Our objectives are bigger than any one individual. Our aim is the prosperity and well-being of all the people of the Third World.'

'So, we don't have to care about the First World at all?'

'That ... well, maybe we can think about that after the revolution.'

'But how will we let the world know that I have become black?'

'What do you think the TV and the internet are here for? The whole world will know in a single day! And with that, everyone will be able to present their complaints directly to you. A beautiful world without the need for middlemen.'

'But will people believe it? I might be Karthav, but even I will burn my fingers if I play with faith.'

'You must make them believe. You did that once two thousand years ago, didn't you? I bet you have some more tricks up your sleeve. Besides, things are much easier these days. People believe whatever you tell them. Just remember one thing – play your cards carefully, safely. Don't expect me to climb on to the cross with you, revolution or no revolution.'

And to test whether Karthav Eesho Mishiha still possessed His old powers, Maria handed him a bottle of water. It was true! The water began to change colour! Maria and Karthav drank the colour-changed water, snacked on mixture, and continued planning the revolution. In the middle of all this, Karthav forgot all about what He had come to talk about.

Since then, whenever He is bored, Karthav comes looking for Maria. He believes Maria when she says that He will be the hero of the revolution of all the oppressed people of the world. He knows that the revolution He had started two thousand years ago has come to nothing, understands that the world has remained the same two thousand years later. So, He comes to Maria every now and then to remind her, 'Listen, this revolution, let's get on with it as quickly as possible. I'm excited!'

Maria too wants to begin the revolution with Karthav Eesho Mishiha as its leader as quickly as possible. But things have to come together, don't they?

'Yeah, well, something miraculous has to happen if there is to be a revolution here.'

'We can make miracles. That's what I am here for, isn't it?'

'Uvva! Like that's going to happen!'

'What? Haven't I walked on the sea? Changed water into wine?'

'There you go again, on and on about the sea and the wine, every time someone mentions the word "miracle". Listen, we don't need the help of a god to change water into wine. We have the technology for it. And we don't need a god who boasts about walking on water. What we need is a god who will do something for those who are struggling. But what's the point? What else can we expect from a god who cursed the fig tree when it didn't set fruit!'

'To tell you the truth, I am more than a little ashamed of that particular episode. I was quite silly to behave like that. What happened was that I was very hungry and, well, lost my control.'

'Even my Kuncheriya valyappachan, who was probably the most devout person on earth, had his doubts about it. Do you run into him up there?'

'How would I recognize your Kuncheriya valyappachan? Up there, they are all the same, Kuncheriyas, Devassys, Varkis, Johns, Aips, Mathayis ... The same expressions, the same doubt-filled eyes ... How I wish I could just leave that place forever! One time, on 25 December, I was so bored – you must remember that's the day Christians the world over get drunk and debauched in my name – and I asked them, "Hey, what about having a party? Let's also be jolly." Ambambo! The look they gave me! I just went off and curled into a corner and went to sleep.'

'I bet now you feel we humans should have remained monkeys.'

'But humans were never monkeys! I created humans as humans and monkeys as monkeys. I see this all the time! Humans do hundreds of years of research and come up with some utter crap. Just think about it, will you? Do I need to create monkeys and then wait for centuries to create humans out of them? Could I not create monkeys and humans at the same time? If I can create monkeys, why wouldn't I be able to create humans? Such foolishness!'

At that point, Maria asks Karthav Eesho Mishiha something that questions the very existence of all gods.

'Tell me, do you gods really have the kind of power that humans believe you have?'

Maria genuinely hopes that gods exist, desires it with all her heart, except that they should be gods who know how to do their jobs properly. What is the point in having gods who can't even stop humans killing each other? The idea of a living, breathing, laughing, crying human being who could, without an iota of regret, plunge a weapon into the body of another human being just like him often makes Maria weep. Why is he incapable of realizing that he is murdering another being who has the same emotions, desires, joys and sorrows? Whenever she thinks about this, Maria wonders whether Hobbes was right when he said 'Man is basically a beast by nature'. Maria does not understand why nations are only too ready to sacrifice their citizens in the name of utterly inhospitable deserts and lands buried under snow. She fails to understand the psychology of nations and human beings who create borders between lands, saying, 'This is mine; that's yours.' In short, the ethics of this world, its humans and its gods are beyond Maria's comprehension.

Nimmi has been trying, for a while now, to make a bunch of red plastic flowers, placed on a tall stool covered with a piece of red satin cloth, disappear. The stool and the flowers were purchased specifically for this purpose, and the satin cloth was a piece of sexy lingerie she owned. Every time she fails to make the flowers disappear, Nimmi curses in English – 'Shit!' Instead of the skimpy dresses she usually wears, Nimmi is dressed in a voluminous gown with big pockets and appliqued with sun and stars and various other objects in space. The gown, too, was bought for this specific purpose. These days, Nimmi is doing a correspondence course in magic. Every Monday, the postman delivers a pile of books with the picture of the magician who is the trainer and owner of the magic school on their covers. Nimmi has effortlessly left her sexuality research and landed on magic. In her opinion, magic is a great art.

'Nimmi, did you know, my grandfather was a magician,' Maria tells her.

'The one you visit all the time?'

'He is "is", not "was". I said "was".'

'Oh. I thought that was a grammatical mistake. Who is this other grandfather?'

'A great-grandfather who lived nine generations ago. Chirammel Kathanar. If he were alive today, you could have learned magic from him.'

'His magic would be outdated now. I guess if he were alive today, no one would even call him a magician.'

'Magic is magic, always. And given how clever my grandfather was, he would have easily learned all the new technologies.'

Maria is pissed off that Nimmi has belittled her ancestor's ability and decides not to talk to her again. But soon, she is bored.

'So, aren't you doing anything in sexuality any more?'

'I've stopped it for now,' says Nimmi, 'but I will take it up again soon. If I learn magic, I can apply that to my sexual adventures. If I become good at it, I might even be able to sleep with a man while his wife is asleep on the other side. What fun, imagine! But once I learn magic, I'm going to return to America. This land is useless. People here consider sleeping with another woman's husband a major crime!'

'If I knew magic, I would make a lot of money.'

'You don't need to know magic to make money. Magic is meant for more difficult things.'

'It is the easiest way to make money, though. I didn't ask to be one, but all my life, I've been a daridravasi, always broke. Didn't try not to be, I guess.'

Nimmi goes back to practising magic tricks. Bored, Maria walks up to the roof, resolving to think for a bit. She keeps sighing long and deep; there are a lot of things she needs to sigh about.

It is evening, and the sun is disappearing. Fed up with sighing about her life, Maria decides to think about the sun who is on his way to wake up Americans. If he doesn't get there on time, Americans won't wake up and America will be in deep trouble. And not just America, the whole world. The economy, the stock market – everything will be in trouble.

But, according to Lily teacher, the sun stayed where it was, and it was the earth that revolved around it. That means, in about twelve hours, she will be where America is now, Maria thinks. If someone were to build a shed in the sky and look down, they will see Maria where George Bush was twelve hours ago. And what if Maria is in the shed? The whole world will pass before her, just like when she had sat watching Appachan chasing Neenanty around the house all those years ago. Where there was Africa, there will be Antarctica in a few hours. But will it really be possible to see the poles? Africans, Chinese people, white-skinned sahibs – everyone will go revolving before her, calling out, 'Good morning, Maria!'

# 17

# Kottarathil Veedu, Appachan and Ammachi

'Appacha, every time I think of Chandi, I feel like crying.'

Maria is sitting on the floor on the veranda of Kottarathil Veedu, and Geevarghese is in his easy chair. Maria is talking to Geevarghese, but it is Mariyamma who answers.

'You're completely mad! You were mad when you were five years old, you're mad when you're thirty, and you'll be mad when you're sixty. It's all your appachan's fault. He's the one who made you like this.'

Geevarghese gives Mariyamma a stern look, but decides it is better not to say anything to this woman who, even though she is his wife, is completely foolish. Seeing his expression, Mariyamma hesitates but continues nevertheless.

'It's like them old folk used to say! She wants to cry it seems, thinking about some old dog that used to hang around the house! That too a dog that thought too much of itself. Susanna was right when she said children should be brought up by their mother and father. This, see, this is what happens if they're brought up by their grandfather!'

Mariyamma invokes 'them old folk' as evidence to the truth of everything she says. Everything, or at least ninety-five per cent, of what she says starts with 'like them old folk used to say'. It is just a habit. People who lived a long time ago have nothing to do with anything she says. How would they know what Maria feels when she thinks about Chandippatti?

'Look at your siblings,' Mariyamma continues. 'Look how well they live. How they bring joy and peace and comfort to their parents.'

'How, Ammachi?'

'Take Mathew for instance. Isn't he a big doctor in America?'

'How is that of any use to his parents? It's only of use to Americans.'

'See, this is what's wrong with you. You only think crooked thoughts. See everything topsy-turvy.'

'So, what about Anne and Lisa then? How are they of benefit?'

'Anne and Lisa? They got married at the proper time and had children at the proper time for their parents to enjoy in their old age.'

'Ammachi, everyone can make a child. It's not that hard. If you want, I can step out for half an hour and come back prepared to have a child in a few months. I don't even have to work hard for it. Any man can do the work. So, don't try to put me down talking about having children. Besides, where is the fairness in what you say? If a man has a good job, he is considered accomplished, even if he doesn't have any children. But for a woman to be considered accomplished, she just has to produce some children.

She can go to Pluto and back, and still you won't acknowledge her accomplishment unless she has popped out a few children. Truly, Ammachi, I don't understand your world or its standards!'

Even as Maria is speaking, even before she gets her second sentence out, Mariyamma is shouting, 'Shut UP, shut UP!' and when Maria continues speaking, Mariyamma puts her hands to her ears, refusing to listen. She glares at Geevarghese who is sitting there laughing.

'The girl is spouting nonsense and you laugh!' she screams. 'How can you laugh? Does anyone else in this world say such things?'

'She is right though, isn't she? She should have been born in some other world, not this one…' Geevarghese says, partly to Mariyamma and partly to himself.

'So true, Appacha!' Maria says. 'You and me, both of us should have been born somewhere else. If we were born in Brazil, they would have made you president!'

Everyone falls silent for a while. Then, Maria returns to the past.

'Remember how Chandi ran after you when you chased Neenanty around the house that time? Every time I think of it, I can't stop laughing.'

'What? Nothing like that happened, ever!' Mariyamma and Geevarghese respond in unison.

'You must have dreamt it,' Mariyamma continues. 'This is what it has come to. The girl can't tell what is real and what is dream! It's all down to how you were brought up. What else!'

Geevarghese watches Maria's eyes welling up. 'It might have happened,' he says. He pauses for a while and continues, 'Something like that has happened.'

Maria understands that Appachan is saying this to console her. It only increases her sadness, and she walks out of the house.

Compared to its old appearance, Kottarathil Veedu has a greyish look now, but its 'garden' is still well looked after. Mariyamma is fond of flowers and plants. She is fond of the house too, but she liked it better when it was full of people. Now that it is empty, her enthusiasm for looking after it has waned.

There is a section set aside entirely for anthuriums. Every time she sees an anthurium bloom, Maria is reminded of men's 'shoo'. If it wasn't for that, Maria might have liked men better, whereas Nimmi likes men because of it and Aisha loathes it and its owners.

Mariyamma's 'garden' is an example of the fine balance between tradition and modernity. Traditional plants like pichi, mulla, chembakam, the four-o-clock plant, hibiscus and pavizhamalli bob their heads right alongside modern varieties like orchid, gerbera, petunia and chrysanthemum. Roses of both kinds – traditional and modern – although with the arrival of newcomers in yellow, orange and magenta, the old roses in red and pink have lost their lustre. Still, they hold their heads high, saying, 'We too are roses.' Kottarathil Veedu had flowering plants even before Mariyamma's arrival. But pichi, mulla, chembakam and hibiscus did not a 'garden' make – they only made a yard with flowers. This was a long time ago. Maria had not been born yet.

Maria looks at the black pepper vines clambering up coconut trees. 'Let's say a coconut tree brings in an income of a hundred rupees. But a coconut tree with a pepper vine clambering all over it brings in five hundred rupees. That is the economics of it,' Maria remembers.

Maria walks through the rubber plantation and reaches the pond. In the olden days, it had been full of fish even if they were only tilopi. Now there are only frogs. When she was a child, their karyasthan Ittan had told Maria that the white foam that floated on the water were frog eggs. Maria had been doubtful. 'How can eggs be like foam?' She still has her doubts. When she was a child, Maria had thought that the pond was huge. But now that she has grown up, she understands that it is not that big after all.

# 18

# Maria's Scattered Thoughts, Dreams, Life

Aravind is not someone who has the capability or the inclination to deceive anyone. Still, when he thinks about Maria, something sticky rises up from his heart, something like guilt.

You are like a sister to me ... Aravind tried to convince Maria, and himself. And yet, the way his heart beats when she is near...

The shiver that runs down his body when he touches her...

The way his gaze slips towards her body...

The heady fragrance that is all hers...

All of it troubles and energizes him at the same time. So, why not acknowledge what he feels?

This is what Aravind thinks whenever he looks at Maria:

*O my Lord, O my Lord, how much I love her! She, the only woman I want to hold close to my heart. God is witness to the amount of tears I have shed thinking about us, me and her! The moment I lose her will be the single most significant moment in my life. I have often thought what I will say when she leaves me, and it always comes to this: My Maria! She is super nice! For Maria, everything is 'super' – super nice*

*... super emotional ... super fragile ... super funny ... super crazy ... And me? I'm just a normal man. Super normal, in Maria's words. When I try to remember all the intimate moments in my life, Maria is present in each of them. If I desired to share myself with anyone, it would only be Maria. But what, then, of my life? No, never. Like I said, I am just a normal man.*

That is the problem. If he had felt the way he did with any woman other than Maria, Aravind would have acknowledged it. A hundred times over. But Maria ... To think about marrying her and taking her home ... It is great to be friends with someone who keeps harping on about an ancestor who taught magic to Kadamattathu Kathanar or about Karthav Eesho Mishiha who sought her company because He was bored. But marrying such a person...

There is something else. Maria had fallen in love with someone and married him, only to leave him after six months for no particular reason. 'This is not what I want,' that was all she said. Aravind cannot even imagine the thought of Maria leaving him declaring *he* is not what she wants.

That is the real issue.

Aravind had once asked Maria about her short-lived married life, and she said she didn't remember anything. When Aravind pressed her, she said, 'Honestly, I would tell you if I remembered. My marriage is a file that has been permanently deleted from my brain.' From that day on, Aravind has lived with the fear that he, too, would be deleted from her brain one fine day.

Maria is thinking about Geevarghese and how he made arrack from cashew fruits...

*Until the arrack he brewed with his own hands in his own compound was all drunk, Geevarghese would move his bed out into* the yard, spending his nights there in the company of Kelan and Velayudhan. During cashew season, when Maria went to pick cashew nuts with Mariyamma, she would keep aside plump, juicy fruits for Geevarghese's arrack brewing. Nuts for Ammachi and fruits for Appachan!

Eetha was praying. When the rest of the family said their prayers in the evenings, Eetha would be too busy in the kitchen. So, she prayed alone afterwards.

'Our Bava who art in heaven! Hallowed be thy name ... on earth as it is in heaven...'

'Eetha, my dear, if earth became like heaven, where the hell would I plant my yam and taro?' The question was from Velayudhan, who was romping on the bed in the yard with Geevarghese and Kelan, their stomachs full of arrack.

In response, Eetha picked up the broom and chucked it at him.

'Oh, it all happened such a long time ago!'

With some difficulty, Aravind withdraws his gaze from Maria's breasts and looks at her face.

'What all?'

'Ey, nothing,' Maria says, 'I was just remembering the old days.'

'Why do you carry these things that happened in the past everywhere like a bundle? I feel like you are a person from the past. Not just your past, but the past in general.'

'The past is fascinating, though, don't you think? There would be princes and magicians and ghosts and kuttichathans ... Such fun! Aravind, listen, could we go somewhere far away and live?'

'But how will we live?'

'Every time I come up with a good idea, you ask some lame question. Is *living* such a difficult thing? All the people all over the world live, don't they?'

'Yes, but they all *do* something in order to live.'

'We will too. We could do yard work for someone. And when we make enough money, we could buy some land, lots and lots of land. We could cultivate that land, keep goats and cows and chicken, even an elephant if possible! And people will say, "Let's buy our vegetables from Maria" and "Maria's vegetables are super fresh and super nice!" and "Let's buy our milk from Maria" and "The milk from Maria is super tasty and super white!"'

As she says these things to Aravind, Maria is under the impression that she is deeply in love, not with Aravind but with someone else. The honest truth is that Maria is confused about who she is in love with at any given time. This person, that person or that other person? By the time Maria thinks about it and comes to a conclusion, this person, that person and that other person will all have gone their own way. To Maria, love is as confusing as the thing with Becker and Federer. When Becker gave up playing, Maria cried continuously for four days, and on the fifth day, she made a decision: 'I will not love any other tennis player like I loved Becker.' For a while, Maria was able to stick to her promise, but then Federer beat Becker in straight sets, got to the top and sat there. Even now, on occasion, Maria finds her infidelity shocking. Aravind does not like tennis. He believes it is a game of rich people, and that since Maria is poor, she should not watch this game.

Aravind has been silent witness to so many of Maria's love affairs. Each time a love affair came to an end, Maria fell into Aravind's arms and wept, and each time he consoled her as best he could. Poor Aravind. After she ended one such relationship, in one of their drinking sessions, her lover wiped his eyes and said, 'She is mad, truly mad, poor thing.'

Exhausted from weeping, when Maria went into the kitchen, Aisha was making toast with jam.

'Aisha, can I have some toast?'

'But you don't like toast.'

Maria ate five slices of toast smeared with jam. 'Aisha, toast is so tasty,' she said. 'I am amazed that I thought I didn't like bread all this time.'

'What did you have against bread?'

'Oh, that. When I got divorced, I was broke, remember? I slept in this tiny little room on a mat on the floor. And all I had to eat was bread – a single loaf over three days. It went on for some time, and then I took a decision. I made myself vomit all the bread I had eaten up until that moment.'

'And?'

'And what? I went to Appachan and Ammachi. And ate Ammachi's appam and chicken curry until I was full.'

Maria waits for Aravind at the beach. Aravind organizes these trips to the beach as a ruse to be alone with Maria, without Hari and Vinayakan hanging around. It is the tourist season and the beach is crowded. Local vendors pursue white tourists with handicrafts they assume they would like and, of course, also to ogle at the madammas and to scope a chance to touch them if possible. Most tourists buy their wares assuming that this is what tourists are supposed to buy when visiting this country, while others buy them just to get rid of the vendors. But will the vendors go away? The same vendor will appear before the same tourist within half an hour. Some vendors think that the tourist won't be able to recognize them, while others end up selling to the same tourist because they couldn't tell one white-skinned tourist apart from another. In either case, it is the tourist who gets harried in the process. No one pursues the local tourists, no one pays them any attention.

Maria watches a dog walking along with a madamma. It is obvious that there is a warm relationship between the dog and the woman. Every now and then, the dog raises his eyes and looked at the madamma with deep love and affection, and licks the white-white woman's white-white shin. And each time he does it, the madamma kisses his snout.

Suddenly, a local man approaches them. From the look the dog gives him, it is clear that he knows the man and hates him. The madamma hugs the dog tightly, passes the leash to the man along with some money, and walks away looking back over her shoulder several times. The dog refuses to move and begins howling until, finally, the man drags him away by his leash.

'Looks like the dog has taken to the madamma,' Maria says as they pass before her.

'Yes. Look at him, all fat and glowing.'

'How much money did she give you to look after her dog?'

'This is my dog, not hers.'

'You're lying!'

'No, I'm not! It's the truth!'

'So, why does the madamma love your dog so much then?'

'She took my dog on rent for a week. See, over there? That's my house. The madamma was walking past one day when the dog barked. He's a dog, so he'll bark, won't he? But this madamma, she came into the house saying the dog called her. Stared at his face for a while, and you know what she said? She said this dog was her husband from her past life! Crazy! But then, most madammas are crazy. Anyway, she began making a right old ruckus, wanting to take him with her. Finally, I said she can have him. Then she says she has to return to America in a week, so she'll borrow him until then. She really wanted to take him with her to America, but what to do, it is very difficult for Indian dogs to get American visas. They think it might be a security risk. She has promised him that she will be back soon.'

'So, how much money did she give you?'

'She said she'll give me two thousand rupees for a week. I said that was too little. She said two thousand was too much money to rent a dog for a week. So, I said, to me, this is a dog, but to you, it is your husband, and two thousand is too little for a husband. Finally, we agreed on three thousand and five hundred rupees.'

Maria is angry with the dog that forgot his loyalty the moment he saw the white-skinned madamma. Even dogs are looking for opportunities to piss off to America! What chance then for the Third World revolution!

Stalls selling fish, caught and cooked on the spot, are doing a brisk business. White tourists stand in front of them with their pale eyes oozing with desire trained on the fish that are turning into curry. The locals stay away – our crabs and prawns are meant only for foreigners after all.

Fish and prawns, destined to be white folk's dinner, dance in the buckets of water displayed in front of the stalls. Their eyes reflect the bewilderment in finding their world suddenly diminished, and they die with their eyes full of incomprehension and confusion. Those who eat them do not look into their eyes, and so are oblivious to the traces of confusion still in them, even after death. Maria remembers the pot of fish curry Ammachi had thrown away because there was fear in the fishes' eyes even after being cooked. A potful of terrified-fish curry!

Boats return from the sea; fishermen pile up the fish right on the shore and begin selling them. Fresh fish with gleaming underbellies. Maria had seen a particular kind of fish on TV a long time ago, fish that swam all the way from the ocean and up certain rivers to their sources in order to lay their eggs in a specific spot. We might wonder, 'Oh, look, they have reached their destination after so much trouble!' But no! Their troubles have only begun. The next thing they have to do is to swim up a waterfall from down below. As we watch them, we think, 'There can't be anything harder than that! This surely must be their last predicament.' That is when we see a battalion of bears, waiting for them at their destination with their arms outstretched. Maria thinks that the only reason Karthav created them was to suffer. Since fish are, on the whole, a foolish species, almost all of them jump right into the arms of the bears. Only a handful successfully evade them, twisting their bodies out of reach or changing direction at the last minute, and reach their destination. And once there, they stand on one fin and lay their eggs, and promptly die. After taking all this risk! Some keep looking over their shoulder to watch out for bears even as they lay their eggs. Little do they know that, bears or no bears, their lives are about to end as soon as they finish laying their eggs. Still, not a single fish shows enough intelligence to observe what is happening around them, to understand that laying eggs means certain death, and go back without laying the eggs. Couldn't they lay their eggs somewhere less risky, at least once? Was swimming up waterfalls and running the gauntlet of bears the only way their eggs would come out?

Maria is overcome with the fear that Appachan is getting more and more unwell. There are other worries too. Federer has begun to lose almost all his matches. Her lover has left her. And

Aravind refuses to listen to her no matter how much she pleads with him to go somewhere far away to live. So, Maria weeps almost all of the time.

Aisha decides to throw her a party to take her mind off these things. Maria does not quite understand the difference between a party and their normal drinking sessions, but Aisha says there is a difference. On normal days, their drinking sessions are clandestine affairs, scared as they are that Saralachechi will find out what they are up to, even though there is nothing to fear from her as she nods off and sleeps like a buffalo in the middle of watching her 9 p.m. serial. On party days, Aisha powders up a couple of sleeping pills and puts it in Saralachechi's food. They could then turn the whole house upside down and Saralachechi would be none the wiser. So, party days mean having the freedom to drink as much as they want, and dance and laugh and scream and bawl to their hearts' content.

Radhika does not partake in boozing or smoking, so she goes off to bed early. Drinking, smoking, wearing skimpy clothes like Nimmi – these are all unforgivable crimes in Radhika's estimation. She is always anxious about things like virginity and hymen. Aisha says that Radhika even walks slowly and carefully, worried as she is about rupturing her hymen. Maria knows she is exaggerating. Maria, Aisha and Nimmi have never had such fears. Aisha is of the opinion that what can rupture needs to rupture, and Nimmi thinks she must have been born with a ruptured hymen. And Maria … Maria isn't even sure that such a thing exists.

Nimmi is puffing on the charas. It is Vinayakan who supplies her top quality charas that he procures in the Himalayas. Maria did not know they had such a relationship or how it began because, as far as she is aware, Aisha and Nimmi knew Vinayakan only as Maria's friend. At first, Maria wondered whether Vinayakan was a partner in Nimmi's sexuality research. Then she remembered that Vinayakan was not the type to make all that effort because, well, it took effort. Maria is in full agreement with Vinayakan on this. This thing, sex, it is only men who have never experienced it who give it so much importance. All the men and women Maria knows have complete sexual freedom, and because of it, none of them take it all that seriously. It is so everywhere in the world where there is sexual freedom. When they did a survey in America, the majority of the men said they would rather have a good cup of coffee than sex.

Plastered, Nimmi telephones Nimish – the son of their neighbour Makarandan chettan and an active partner in her sexuality research – and asks him to come over. Nimish appears at their first-floor door soon enough, shimmying up the mango tree by the side of the house as usual. Maria does not like Nimish. He has a sickly look with bulging muscles and a smug 'I am so handsome' expression on his face. And that pretentious name! Every night, Makarandan chettan takes off his clothes and walks around naked in his room, exposing himself to them, never suspecting, even in his dreams, that his son is with them at the time. An outraged Aisha wanted to inform Saralachechi and put an end to it, but Nimmi stopped her saying that watching Makarandan's naked parade helped her achieve 'better orgasms'. So, Aisha abandoned the idea. She is always supportive in such matters.

In the beginning, Maria had assumed that Aisha was a lesbian, and when she realized this wasn't so, Maria asked her why she didn't consider becoming one. Aisha said she couldn't, because even though she felt mentally and emotionally close to women, she did not feel physical attraction. Maria feels the opposite, thinks it is easier to feel physically close to women. Who doesn't like sucking boobs!

Sexuality research done, Nimish goes away, shimmying down the mango tree.

'I am going to have a baby with him,' Nimmi says, coming out of her room.

Aisha's jaw drops. 'But isn't he only around twenty or so?' she asks after a while. 'And you're nearing forty!'

'Yes, he is in his prime years. And damn healthy. That's why I chose him. The baby will be healthy too.'

'And are you going to live together?' Aisha asks.

'Of course! We'll be living together as husband and wife.'

'For the life of me, I can't imagine Makarandan chettan as your father-in-law.' That is all Maria has to say in the matter.

Anyway, a couple of days later, Nimish is missing. Try as she might, Nimmi cannot find out anything about the whereabouts of her future husband. She walks up and down, calling out, 'Nimish, darling.' To stop Nimmi, who is only a few years younger than his wife, from becoming his daughter-in-law, Makarandan chettan has packed Nimish off, first to his brother-in-law in Bombay and from there to the Gulf. Nimmi goes to his gate and asks in her American accent, 'Is Nimish in, Makeraanten chetta?' 'Spoil innocent little children, will you, you shameless bitch,' says Makarandan chettan in response, but Nimmi does not understand him. Nimmi usually does not hear what others say, especially if it is in Malayalam. In any case, soon after, Nimmi finds another bulgy-muscled man and decides to have a baby with him instead.

As Aisha says, it will be a miracle if Nimmi doesn't leave the child somewhere and go on her way, oblivious.

Nimmi thrusts her fingers down her throat and vomits everything she has drunk till then, and begins to get drunk again from scratch. She does this often – drinking until her tummy is about to burst and, feeling unsated still, making herself vomit so she can drink again. She vomits easily anyway, what with drinking way more than she should, mixing up alcohols and brands, and to top it all off, eating all the old and spoiling food that is in the fridge. Aisha never gets rid of old food, just sticks it into the fridge saying, 'Nimmi will eat it.'

Of all the people Maria knows, Aisha is the most decent drunk. She takes her time, drinking each drink slowly, sip by sip, accompanying it with the weirdest of snacks – fruit, salad, cheese and so on, like white people. Three or maximum four – Aisha never has more drinks. So, Maria has never seen her plastered or vomiting. Now, Aisha has gone to bed and Nimmi is wasted, and Maria is alone. She thinks of Aravind … and about the farm they are going to start.

Breathlessly, Maria talks to Karthav Eesho Mishiha, non-stop, about the beautiful farm she and Aravind are going to set up. Karthav has come to her to tell her that He is now fully prepared to start the revolution they had planned and that they should get on with it immediately, but here she is, going on and on about some farm.

'Is the revolution more important to you, or this dookly Aravind?' He asks, irate. ('Dookly' is a word Karthav has learned from Maria. He has picked up many such made-up words from her. One time, bored to tears listening to them reading the Bible in heaven – all they did there was read the Bible – Karthav had blurted out: 'Can't you put the stupid kunthappanaatti down for a while and give us all a bit of peace and quiet!' An old man who looked like a grandfather had come forward from among the Bible readers, given Karthav a stern look, and said, 'If I'd known this is what you were like, I would not have put myself through all the trouble for a hundred years down there.' That old man was Kuncheriya.)

'I was thinking,' says Maria, 'what if I marry Aravind?'

# 19

# The Dream that Is Kuttappayi

For the first time, Maria feels the presence of death in that body. Shocked, Maria releases Geevarghese from her hug and sits down on the floor.

'You felt it, didn't you? Death?'

'Why are you talking like this, Appacha?'

'I felt your shock when you hugged me. Don't worry, these days I am always ready to die. I'm at an age when the body is a burden for the man. Besides, Mathiri valyammachi will be waiting for me. Kelan, Velayudhan, and Kali too. To tell you the truth, I am even looking forward to seeing my appan again, if you can believe it. You watch, we'll have such a party up there. My only concern is you, Maria. You must start living properly now, stop floating through life like this. I want to go knowing that your life is peaceful.'

'You won't die … Appachan won't die … I won't let you die!'

'Why can't you marry Aravind?'

'I like him very much, Appacha, but I don't think he likes me. He doesn't like me. He doesn't want to marry me. Oh, please …

please ... please ... if only Aravind liked me a little ... Don't die, Appacha. I won't let you die!'

It is the sight of Maria sitting on the floor and bawling that welcomes Mariyamma when she walks in from the rubber plantation. Someone must have died, she thinks at first, at the same time acknowledging that her husband, the next in line to die among her nearest and dearest according to her calculations, is sitting quietly in his chair. No one else is at an age to die.

'What is it? What happened?' Mariyamma asks, gathering Maria up in her old but still strong arms.

Still sobbing, Maria is unable to answer, so it is Geevarghese who answers.

'She doesn't want me to die, that's why she's crying.'

Geevarghese says this laughing, but Mariyamma sits on the ground, suddenly tired. 'Molly,' she calls in a feeble voice, looking through the door to the interior of the house, 'bring me my BP medicine.'

Mariyamma takes the medicine Molly brings her and waits until she is sure it has started working.

'Everyone dies,' she says. 'I'll die, you'll die, your appachan will die. That's not such a big deal. You'll frighten us to death, carrying on like this.'

She sits silently for a few minutes. Then, exclaiming, 'Aiyo! Lunchtime is almost here and I haven't even started thinking about what to cook,' she gets up and goes inside. Geevarghese sits in his easy chair with the same smile on his face. Maria runs out into the compound, still sobbing.

In among the trees, Maria runs into Karthav Eesho Mishiha and makes an agreement with him.

'Appachan must not die … My appachan must not die! I know everyone has to die some day, but not my appachan. Don't pacify me like Aravind does, saying Appachan will be with us for a long time yet and so on. I refuse to compromise on the promise of "a long time". Appachan's death must be removed, permanently. That's the only request I will make in my entire life to you, to whatever system is up there deciding these things.'

Maria is making these demands of Karthav, sitting on top of the cashew tree on which she used to play 'bus driving' as a child. From that vantage point, she can see the whole compound, the road that passes through the compound cutting it in two (in Maria's childhood, this was just a mud lane) and Ammachi's cows and goats grazing in the compound. As she sits there, Maria sees someone far away, walking towards her with something hanging from his hand. As he comes near, Maria sees that what he has in his hand is fish, freshly caught varaal strung in a bunch using coconut leaf spine. The sight of the varaal makes Maria's mouth water – the curry cooked with kodampuli and eaten a day later … Ho! When he reaches the tree on which Maria is sitting, the man with the varaal looks up. He is beautiful, with very dark skin … Joy and surprise light up his face simultaneously when he sees her perched on the tree, and in a voice filled with surprise, overflowing with joy, he says her name: 'Maria!'

Maria is mortified that a full-grown man has caught her sitting on the tree, but she continues to sit there firmly in order to hide her embarrassment.

'Who are you? I'm not sure I recognize you…' Maria says, looking down at the man.

The full-grown man looks at her with the joy still on his face. 'Don't recognize me? I'm Kuttappayi.'

Maria feels like she is about to fall off the tree in a dead faint. The object of her first ever love is standing below with the most beautiful smile in the whole world! And here she is, sitting on top of a cashew tree! Maria adjusts her clothes, clutches the branch and sits still.

Minutes tick by, and faced with Maria's continued silence, the beauty of Kuttappayi's smile begins to fade. Maria cannot risk it losing all its beauty, so she speaks.

'How did you know it was me?'

The smile comes back to Kuttappayi's face in full glory. 'Every time I pass this way, I look up. This is where you used to be when I brought you ainippazham, remember?' Then, after a pause, he continues, 'Exactly as you're sitting now!'

Kuttappayi gives Maria a look that takes in her whole body. Blushing, Maria realizes that the love you feel at seven years old and at thirty years old is one and the same.

'I always ask Appachan about…' Kuttappayi pauses, not sure how to address Maria, and then continues, '… Maria.'

Maria is hoping to hear him say 'girl' but Kuttappayi is embarrassed to call this full-grown woman 'girl'.

'You got married, your appachan said…'

Maria wonders why Kuttappayi is talking about such uninteresting things, especially at this moment when she is so smitten. So, to change the subject, Maria says:

'You still catch fish?'

'Of course! All the time! Here, take these varaal. Ask Ammachi to cook them for you.'

'Still pick ainippazham?'

'Ey, no!' Shyness spreads over Kuttappayi's face as he says this. 'No one else has asked me for ainippazham since … I think of you whenever I see an aini tree.'

Maria wants to laugh. What a tree to think about when in love!

Since Maria is drowning in her love, it is Kuttappayi who speaks, that too intermittently.

Back home, Maria tells Appachan and Ammachi about running into Kuttappayi.

'You must be mistaken,' Mariyamma says. 'Kuttappayi has been in the Gulf for many years now.'

Watching all the stars in Maria's face vanish suddenly, Geevarghese intervenes. 'Must have come home on holidays,' he says. 'I remember Sumathi saying something about it.'

Later, with the same stars in her eyes, Maria tells Aravind about her meeting with Kuttappayi. Aravind has always – meaning from the time Maria first told him about Kuttappayi – hated him, more than he hated Maria's real lovers. 'Him and his confounded varaal! Son of a bitch!' Aravind thinks, but what he says out loud is this:

'And did you cook the varaal?'

'No! I forgot to take it from him...'

Maria wonders why Aravind is talking about the fish when she is telling him such a beautiful love story. Killjoy Aravind!

# 20

# Hari's Departure, and Vinayakan's

And then one day, Hari dies. Falls down in a faint and dies, like they say in the newspapers. They are arguing as usual, Hari and Vinayakan, about some country somewhere that Maria has not even heard about. Maria and Aravind are not really paying attention. After eating all the peanuts off the floor, Maria is busy looking to see if there is anything else strewn around, and Aravind's attention is on what lies beyond the open button of her blouse as she bends this way and that searching the floor, worrying, at the same time, that Hari and Vinayakan would look where he is looking. That's when Hari falls. He doesn't really faint, just falls down. Later, Vinayakan will rack his brain to recall what they were saying at the precise moment of Hari's fall but will never be able to remember.

The moment Hari falls, Maria and Aravind are by his side. Vinayakan continues arguing even as Hari is dying, thinking, vainly, that if he provokes him enough, Hari will get up to argue his point of view. Instead, Hari looks at the three of them sorrowfully and dies with that sorrow still in him. An ordinary death devoid of drama.

The doctors say that Hari died of a heart attack. Maria cannot understand this. Why would Hari's heart, that has beaten regularly and normally, decide to stop beating suddenly for no apparent reason? How could Hari's heart behave so callously?

Aravind, Vinayakan and Jayan are all distraught, but they do everything that is to be done. They take Hari's body in an air-conditioned ambulance to his multi-millionaire father. In the ambulance, as she lies against Aravind's chest, Maria feels very cold. When she looks at Hari's face, she can see that Hari is also feeling very cold. On their way back, Maria thinks that Hari will shout at Vinayakan for making him lie in the freezing air-conditioned ambulance. The thought makes her smile even in the midst of her sorrow. But poor Hari is beyond words, beyond arguments. Aravind feels that Maria is too warm even in the cold air of the ambulance. 'That's because it is Hari's warmth too,' she says. 'Hari is inside me now.' Then, after a pause, she says as though making a declaration, 'From now on, I will carry the warmth of two persons.'

After taking Hari to his multi-millionaire father, they come back and drink kattu rum to their hearts' content. Those who want to cry, cry, and those who want to rage, rage. Convinced that Hari will come back from wherever he has gone, Vinayakan keeps glancing at the door, and every time he realizes it is only a thought, he mutters, 'Thayoli betrayed us!' Maria listens to Jayan promising someone that he will sort out whatever it is that needed sorting. 'Now Jayan has someone in heaven too, the only place he didn't have a contact,' she thinks. 'Now he can say with confidence that we have someone there too.'

After Hari's death, no one comes to the room to hang out – other than Maria, Aravind and, occasionally, Jayan. With Hari's death, Vinayakan completes his transformation into Mad Vinayakan. Unadulterated madness, as he himself used to say about other people's madness. It is not surprising that Vinayakan became Mad Vinayakan because, for him, for the last several years, the only thing that constituted the process of 'being alive' was arguing with Hari.

One day, Maria sees Vinayakan on the road and, loudly calling his name, she runs to him and tries to embrace him. His already long hair has grown even longer, and his clothes are more soiled than they usually are. People stare at him because, for them, he is only a madman, and now they stare at Maria who is trying to hug a madman. As Maria reaches for him, Vinayakan thunders, 'Get away from me, dirty woman,' and walks away muttering, 'Thayoli betrayed us!' Those who are ogling laugh, enjoying the show. Maria sits on the road weeping until, luckily, one of their acquaintances comes that way and takes her to Aravind.

After that incident, Maria begins to be terrified of death, especially the death of her appachan which is imminent. Because, what waits on the other side of the door from death is madness. After returning from her encounter with Vinayakan, Maria continues to weep madly, again and again asking Aravind, 'Will Appachan die? Will Appachan die?' Aravind holds her close and cries quietly, cries for his own world that is slipping from his fingers. For a long time, his whole world, his life, has been Maria first, and then Hari and Vinayakan. Now, Hari is dead, Vinayakan is lost to madness, and Maria is also at the entrance to madness. Aravind holds on to his love, tighter and tighter, knowing that it is slipping out of his grasp, knowing that nothing will ever be the same and still hoping for a miracle...

This is how that evening of tears ends:

Maria sits like a baby bird in Aravind's arms and sobs as she begins her journey into the time and place where she loses her mind.

'I know everything is slipping away from us, Aravind,' she says through her sobs. 'But I so wanted to make a life with you, to have your children ... How I wished I could live a normal life like everyone else...'

Aravind kisses her tear-drenched lips. In that moment, he thinks that her lips are exceptionally soft. That is the first time he thinks that way ... and the last.

# 21
# About the Book Maria Wrote, or Is Going to Write

Those are Geevarghese's last few days on this earth. The climax of an entire human life. Maria is convinced that Appachan won't die because she has an agreement with Karthav Eesho Mishiha. Meanwhile, Geevarghese tries to persuade her that the Other World where he is going is a much better world than this one – a world like the one Kelan had dreamed of, where everyone was equal, where there are no haves and have-nots. In his old age, Geevarghese is nostalgic about Mathiri valyammachi, Mathu valyappan, Anna, Kelan, Kali and Velayudhan, even Kuncheriya and Shoshamma. Geevarghese believes firmly in life after death, except that his idea of it is not the same as the one most people have imagined for aeons. In Geevarghese's idea of life after death, there is no heaven or hell, only a peaceful place filled with joy and goodness. As his body begins to become infirm and out of sync with his mind, Geevarghese yearns to get to this Other World. He spends most of his last days on earth in the company of Mathiri valyammachi, Mathu valyappachan, Kelan and others. They come to him often to reminisce about the old days.

Maria and Geevarghese sit under the chempakam tree in the cemetery, looking at their ancestors. It is evening. Geevarghese believes that dead folk favour evenings, that it is their favourite time of day. But Maria doesn't think that is right because evenings make people nostalgic, and it is not logical to think that this will not be so for dead people just because they are dead. Despite his physical ailments, it is Geevarghese who comes up with the idea of a visit to the cemetery. As he gets closer and closer to death, Geevarghese is more and more anxious about Maria.

'Look at these graves! They are in the wrong order, I just noticed,' says Geevarghese. 'Look, my appan and Mathiri valyammachi are side by side. On the other side of Appan is my ammachi, and on this side of Mathiri valyammachi is Mathachan. How will I be able to lie next to Mathiri valyammachi then? The only consolation is that there is some space next to Mathu valyappachan.'

'But Appacha, if you lie next to Mathiri valyammachi, how will I lie next to you when my time comes?'

'I guess there is enough space for both of us next to Mathachan. But how long will I suffer him in the hope that you will come one day? Will you come?'

'Where else will I go, Appacha? No one will have me anywhere else!'

'But you don't believe in the church...'

'It's not a question of belief, Appacha. It is a question of belonging. It's about being with the people we know, in a place we are familiar with. A place where we belong because of who we are, no matter what we do in our lives.'

As he sits looking at the graves, the life he has lived passes in front of Geevarghese's eyes like a parade. Mathiri valyammachi, Mathu valyappachan, Kuncheriya, Shoshamma, Anna valyamma, Kali, Kelan, Velayudhan, Maria ... He even glimpses Mariyamma and his children, even though they did not play important roles in his life. All these people hold pieces of Geevarghese's past, each one with a piece of the jigsaw puzzle that fits perfectly with the pieces the others hold.

Geevarghese feels he is about to lose consciousness. A sense of peace, satisfaction and happiness that he has never experienced in life fills him. He sees Mathiri valyammachi, dressed in a blue chatta and mundu, waiting to welcome him with outstretched arms. But she is on the other side of a light as bright as the sun but without the heat. He has to cross that light to get to her. A single leap, that is all it would take, and eternal happiness would be his. Geevarghese prepares to take the leap, but...

With great difficulty, Geevarghese brings himself back to life because, in his subconscious, he is aware that Maria is all alone.

'Maria, you have to start living like everyone else does. Only then can I go in peace.'

'You're the one who always said that the problem was not with us but with the world. And you're right, you know. The problem is with the world. Everything is so normal here. Why is it that the cat is always the cat, and the mouse is always the mouse? Why is there no Chandi or Ammini or Mathiri valyammachi or Chirammel Kathanar any more? To be so completely normal is so boring!'

'I guess your ammachi is right. I'm the one who made you like this. Maria, if you continue to be this way, who will look after you when I'm gone?'

'Why should anyone look after me? Can't I look after myself?'

Geevarghese wishes to open her eyes, tell her that she is incapable of looking after herself, that he, Aravind, Aisha and others are the ones who looked after her, paid her rent and bought her the things she needed. Then he thinks, with a great deal of sorrow, that Maria will not understand any of it.

Maria, meanwhile, is lost in the memory of the big gooseberry tree that Kuncheriya valyappachan had cut down, the tree that used to produce copious amounts of gooseberries. If it had still been around, Ammachi could have made gooseberry pickle.

'I have a great idea to make money,' Maria says. 'I'm going to write a book.'

'What about?'

'About us! About Mathiri valyammachi and Chirammel Kathanar, about Kuncheriya valyappachan and Anna valyamma, about Appachan, about me! And of course, about Aravind. I'll be the heroine!'

'And how will this book of yours end?'

'You have to ask? It will end with, "And Maria lived happily ever after."'

'How? Whatever the book, it should have some logic to its ending, no?'

'How about this then? "And then Maria lived happily ever after because:

A. Maria got a well-paid job.

B. Maria went abroad (if it is Brazil, it will be super).

C. Maria started a restaurant with Ammachi as the main chef.

D. Maria started a farm and lived with all the animals in the world.

E. Maria married Aravind and was very happy."'

'You can't end a book like that!'

'Why not! You watch, Appacha. People will read this book and say, "Oh, Maria's book … it's super cool."'

As she says this, Maria knows that she will never write such a book. Because, according to Maria, writing books is boring. But Maria will write her book, much later, and she will write it when she is in a place she would never have dreamed of.

Poor Maria.

## In Conversation
SANDHYA MARY AND JAYASREE KALATHIL

P.S.

Insights,
Interviews
&
More …

**Jayasree Kalathil:** The first thing that struck me when I read *Maria Verum Maria* in the original Malayalam is how unique it was in the context of Malayalam literature. I can't remember ever reading a novel quite like it. Could you tell me a little about how it came about?

**Sandhya Mary:** *Maria Verum Maria* was never meant to be a novel. You know how you have all these crazy thoughts in your head while you lead a normal – well, almost normal – life? I just wanted to know how crazy my thoughts or my head could go. So, I started writing these down in the form of notes. It was fun! I thoroughly enjoyed all that craziness, all that humour in *Maria*. There were times I couldn't control my laughter after writing certain parts. And the best part was that, not being a literary work, I was under no pressure to finish it. Then, for a few years, I didn't write anything at all. I even lost some of the small notebooks in which I had written these notes. It never felt like the process of writing a novel. It started as a conversation between me and Jesus. Then I added characters on the way. So, writing *Maria* was like a celebration of everything 'not normal'. There are only two things that I did deliberately or consciously. One, I gave the story a subtle but definitive political touch, and two, I wanted the narrative to be unsystematic, less structured, something that would reflect the thoughts and writing of a scattered mind – after all, it is written by Maria. I am glad that you think it is unique in Malayalam literature, and I know generally what attracted you to *Maria*. But I am curious to know why you chose to translate it.

**JK:** As you know, I have a personal, professional and political interest in this human experience we call 'madness'. In my academic and political work, I have explored representations of madness in our cultural imaginary, in literature, art, cinema and so on. Often, these representations are appalling, discriminatory and downright harmful in the way they depict the world and human experiences as a dichotomy of sanity/insanity or normal/abnormal. Even much-celebrated stories like M.T. Vasudevan Nair's 'Iruttinte Athmaavu' (The Soul of Darkness) or the film *Thaniyavarthanam* depict madness as a curse that follows one through generations, something that is all-consuming, from which there is no escape, something to be hated, feared. There are exceptions too, of course, for instance N. Prabhakaran's stories, some of which are included in *Diary of a Malayali Madman*.

**SM:** Velayudhan in 'Iruttinte Athmaavu' is a realistic representation of how madness was seen in that era. After all, it was written in the 1960s.

**JK:** Yes, of how 'normal' people saw madness or thought of mad people. But the point I am trying to make is that it is told from that very sanist and ableist perspective, even though Velayudhan, the person deemed mad, is given the narrative voice. In our literature, the story of madness is often told from the point of view of what society sees as sanity.

**SM:** Narrating the story of madness from the point of view of the person deemed mad is not that common in our fiction. As you pointed out, the madman Aagi in the title story in *Diary of a Malayali Madman* is an exception. I love that story for its approach towards madness, its humour, and for its politics. The difference between Aagi and Maria is that he recognizes he is mad, whereas for Maria her mental state is the normal state. There are times when Maria is not sure about her mental state, and that is also part of her character – she is generally not too sure about herself or about anything else. She was born with a scattered or a floating mind.

Society will very easily brand you mad or crazy just because you don't live according to its norms and conditions, or it sees you as being different from its conception of normal or from so-called normal people. That is so cruel. Why can't we accept that there is nothing called normalcy? I agree that there might be situations where people need help with emotional or psychological problems that they face. But if a person is happy, or maybe not even that happy, and talks to themselves, who are we to brand them crazy? Or what if I feel like counting crows today? You leave me alone and let me count my crows. I have often felt that if screaming out loud was considered okay in our society, many of us would not end up in psychiatric treatment. I mean, when you are so angry or so pissed off, just scream out loud and let it out!

**JK:** I think what we are talking about is the fact that writing about madness is hard, especially in a socio-cultural context where madness has not always been represented sensitively, where it has been consistently used in literature and films as comic relief or to represent evil or to drive in the message that being mad is equal to being cursed with a life not worth living. And it continues to be used so even by otherwise politically informed people. Did you have access to a political, creative or social community to write so differently about madness? What were your inspirations for these characters?

**SM:** I am from a very 'normal', conservative, Christian family. Everybody lived a normal life and died a normal death. Even as a child, I had this vague idea that I didn't want to live like my parents or like the innumerable aunts and uncles I knew. There was not even a single 'different' person in our locality. I met such people, people who were somewhat different, for the first time in my life while I was doing my master's in journalism at Thiruvananthapuram. It was a bohemian set of people who lived in an old lodge called Karthika. I instantly felt that I belonged to that place. We were all very poor, but we shared everything – weed, booze and money. I got the idea for Hari and Vinayakan's room from Karthika. Apart from that, I don't think that place inspired me in other ways of thinking about madness. Because, outside of that building, most of these people lived a somewhat normal life. But that place provided some kind of solace to me, something like a blanket effect that protected me or kept me away from the outside world. And I knew a few people who were 'branded bhranthans', people who were deemed mad, who were highly creative but different from the rest of us, whose families were giving them psychiatric treatment even though they had brilliant minds!

**JK:** You said earlier that you have given the story a subtle but definitive political message. In my reading, this message was that madness, which is often seen as some sort of fault or deficiency within an individual's psyche or personality, is really about society and how we treat individuals who are different – for whatever reasons – within that society. Madness is our response to problems with living. Throughout my professional life as an activist-researcher in the field of mental health and human rights, this is something I have worked hard to establish. And I think many of those who read *Maria* will understand this way of looking at madness. Often, as we touched upon earlier, in literary representations of madness, the narrative voice is given to the 'normal' or the 'sane'. I found it refreshing that in *Maria* the story is told from the perspective of Maria and Geevarghese, undoubtedly the 'maddest' of the characters.

**SM:** I loved that intermingling in narration. Sometimes both of them narrate the same story at different times from their own perspective. That was kind of an experiment. I thought I would use Geevarghese to give a different perspective to Maria's story. What I am trying to say through Maria and through Geevarghese is this: let everyone live their own lives in their own way. Like I said earlier, don't brand anyone. Be inclusive. Maria, though not deliberately, is trying to deconstruct the existing family system. Society, her family, all expect her to live a normal life, to get married in a conventional way, to have kids, to fit in. I have always wondered, why is it that everybody is living the exact same life? Society should be full of wonderfully different people, living diverse lives. Also, I wanted to touch upon the notion of being 'successful' in life. Every human being is under so much pressure to be successful. We always hear, 'Don't waste your time!' What if I don't want to use it? What if I just want to go through it? I think *Maria* is ultimately about being *verum* Maria – *just* Maria. Maria is also about a just world. At one point in the novel, in her conversation with Karthav Eesho Mishiha, Maria demands a world that is fair to all human beings. At another point, in lashing out at human beings and their behaviour, Chandippatti demands that they make a just world for all animals.

**JK:** Another thing that attracted me to *Maria* is your use of a child's perspective. I am partial to stories that have a child as the protagonist, or stories that are told, at least for the most part, from the point of view of a child. For me, Little Maria is a worthy member of a whole line-up of literary children who are smart and precocious and yet vulnerable and innocent, possessing a well-developed and richly imaginative inner world. I am talking about literary children like Harper Lee's Scout (*To Kill a Mockingbird*), Donna Tartt's Harriet (*The Little Friend*), the young Gerald Durrell in his autobiographical *My Family and Other Animals*. Having written a story with a child as a protagonist myself – Anu in *The Sackclothman* – I am intrigued by the possibilities of storytelling opened up by the perspective of the child, especially a child who, like Maria and the others I've mentioned here, is not conceived of as living a stereotypical family life or childhood. It is hard to find such children in Malayalam literature.

**SM:** Yes, it is not that common. But we do have Annie in Sarah Joseph's *Aalahayude Penmakkal* (Aalaha's Daughters) and the teenager Lucy in another one of her novels, *Maattathi*. And although *The God of Small Things* is an English novel, Arundhati Roy's Rahel is a Malayali kutty! And I've just noticed – they are all girls, including Maria!

Placing a child, Little Maria, as the main narrative perspective, gave me immense creative freedom. The issue with grown-ups is that they think in a certain way, behave in a certain way. You should have a rational, logical explanation for everything. Children don't have to fit into anything. They can be wild, crazy, make up things ... Also, I loved myself as a child, although I hated my childhood. I too grew up with my grandparents, though my grandfather was nothing like the wise Geevarghese. He was just an ordinary guy. I knew him only as my grandfather and never as a person. We never had any conversations like the ones Maria and Geevarghese have in our life, but we liked each other's company in a peculiar, grown-up way. I was his constant companion, but we were more or less silent most of the time! Maybe I filled that silence with my imagination.

**JK:** I read in one of your interviews that you started writing *Maria* in English. As your English translator, I found that interesting. Why did you switch languages? And how was it to then read the novel written in English by someone else?

**SM:** Like many of us, I talk to myself a lot. In the beginning of my twenties, I started thinking in English – perhaps it was to improve my language – and I loved it! I assumed that my 'self-talking English' was good, though there must have been some usage errors. Also, at that time, I was doing lots and lots of translation, from English to Malayalam and vice versa. Like I said, *Maria* was originally written as notes of my thoughts, and so they naturally came out in English. And when I realized that it could be a novel, I switched to Malayalam. The interesting thing is that I was translating many of the parts in the novel into Malayalam from English! It is funny that you were re-translating those parts back into English. So, for me, I had the whole story of *Maria* in English in my head, even the Malayalam parts, and to be frank, I was a little worried about how it would turn out in translation, whether I would like the new Maria. Then again, I am very passive about my writing, and I forgot about it soon. But when I read your translation, it almost felt not translated, almost the same but at the same time a totally independent novel. It was as though the Maria in my head had jumped into yours! Let me mention one particular scene, the scene where Maria meets Mathiri in the two-dimensional, black-and-white heaven while taking Geevarghese's soul to the Other World. This is one of my favourite scenes: one, because they are two mad women from two completely different generations; and two, because it is a place where everyone's dreams are shattered, not just Maria's. Then that scene leads into, merges with, Geevarghese's death. For me, this was one of the most intense and creative episodes in the novel. And the translation has maintained that intensity and creativity to the full.

And that makes me curious about your process of translation. *Maria*, I believe, is written in a very simple language, the simplest imaginable I would say. But it has many instances of playing with language, twisting words, making up words, colloquial usage. I would like to know how you translated these, how difficult or easy the process was for you, what choices you made.

**JK:** That is an interesting question, and one I get asked a lot. Let me just say, first of all, that while a translator often works focused at the level of a single word, getting bogged down with words can also be detrimental. One of my favourite translators, Edith Grossman, who recently passed away, said: 'A translation can be faithful to tone and intention, to meaning. It can rarely be faithful to words or syntax, for these are peculiar to specific languages and are not transferable.' With *Maria*, as with my other translations, my effort was to understand and capture your intention when you made up words or played with words. This I understood primarily as a way of giving Maria a unique voice to match her unique way of being in this world, what you call in the novel her 'Marian' way of being. For instance, Maria likes to use the word 'bhayankara', which can translate into English in many different ways depending on the context, as terrible, terrific, super, awesome, fearsome and so on. Given that Maria also has a certain colloquial Americanism in her speech, I chose to retain 'super'. There are other colloquial or made-up words – 'dookly' and 'kundappanatti', for example – that Maria uses, that others, even Jesus Christ, learn from Maria. I've chosen to retain these as they are because, well, the idea that others learn words and make them part of their speech is how a language acquires new words.

But it is not just Maria who plays with words and syntax in this book. Pretty much every character is at it. I think this is one of the reasons why, even though the book is the story of Maria, the little neglected girl who eventually had to grow up, and all the fascinating, irritating, nurturing, devastating things that happened meanwhile, it is also about a whole community. Maria is surrounded by fascinating characters, both human and animal, and each of these characters is drawn out and developed fully.

Some of them are familiar – we all probably know a Mariyamma toiling alone inside old extended families, or an eccentric Anna valyamma pacing the corridors of a house which is at once her sanctuary and her prison. But the others – like Mathiri valyammachi, who rewrites the Bible, and Chirammel Kathanar, the world-famous magician-priest – are refreshingly unfamiliar in Malayalam literature. You have even given St George the Martyr – Geevarghese Sahada – a new, specifically small-town-Kerala lease of life. And then, of course, there are the non-human characters – Chandippatti, the dog who is a philosopher, and the wily, smart parrot, Ammini.

**SM:** People have asked me if *Maria* is autobiographical. How can it be? I never had a talking dog! I never knew a talking parrot! I don't have a Geevarghese in my family, or a Mathiri valyammachi, or an Anna valyamma, or a Chirammel Kathanar. Maybe a Mariyamma, yes, but as you say, all elderly matriarchs are more or less like Mariyamma. About Geevarghese Sahada, I have been seeing him in that exact posture for years. I mean, sitting on a horse in that same position for so many years ... Naturally you imagine a story for him or about him! It is the same with Jesus Christ, Karthav Eesho Mishiha. I stopped being a believer by the end of my teenage years, but these characters remain in your cultural life, just like Syrian Christian cuisine or carols at Christmas time, or the Christmas star. All those characters and situations came out naturally without much effort on my part.

As for Chandippatti and Ammini, I think I have excellent communication skills with animals. I really talk with them, and they respond too! The kind of special IQ and EQ they have is beyond our understanding. Ammini and Chandippatti, especially, are results of that communication. The idea of Chandippatti came from a totally crazy dog I met briefly at a bus stop. It gives me immense joy to be with cats and dogs. For me, they are family; we don't own them, they own us. They are more part of my life than human beings. And, as with the child protagonist who provides the narrative perspective, animal characters give space for immense creative freedom and imagination.

**JK:** And because of all these people and animals, although the book is about Maria who is 'just Maria', it is also about a community, the story of 'Maria's land' – Kerala – in a specific moment in history, a social commentary on the idea of family and the tenets of patriarchy, and how women – and men – of different generations negotiate its vicious waters. So, I was intrigued by the phrase with which the novel ends – 'poor Maria'. Why so?

**SM:** I am glad you asked that question. That 'poor' is not only meant for Maria, but for every human being who, despite being a beautiful soul, ends up lost or branded as a failure because we suck as a society.

**JK:** You have said somewhere that you found 'the task of having to neatly and systematically convey the ideas inside my head boring', and that you did not publish your first story until the age of thirty. And yet you have published a collection of short stories as well as *Maria*.

**SM:** I never thought about writing fiction until I was thirty, though I always knew I could write! But then, the first story I wrote got published in *Mathrubhumi* weekly, the leading

Malayalam literary magazine. After publishing three or four stories, I almost stopped writing – for no particular reason. I am a very lazy writer. Being creative is one thing, but the process of writing requires much effort and discipline, as you know very well. And my first instinct is to skip it! I have never had that 'I must write this down' kind of feeling about anything. These days I don't write much fiction, only a few short stories. I have a novel in mind, but I postpone writing it!

# Acknowledgements

*Maria, Just Maria* is the story of a woman trying to find her place in a world that is defined in binaries – normal/abnormal, man/woman, natural world/human world, love/hate, life/death – and of family systems based on tradition and legacy, of moral imperatives to be good, of questions to be answered and exams to be passed. In this story, gods plan revolutions with humans, cats printed on knickers have opinions, old women rewrite the Bible. It is probably the first book I have translated in which I found so much of my own story reflected. It made translating this book somehow more personal. It is also a book which was, by the author's own admission, first conceived of in English. A challenging prospect for this translator, as it made me agonize over my own English. But from the first message I sent asking for permission to translate this book, Sandhya Mary was enthusiastic, supportive and engaged. Her sense of humour, generosity of spirit and patience made the whole process fun and interesting. Thank you, Sandhya.

I am thankful for friends like S. Hareesh, Shaji Jacob and E.V. Fathima, without whose advocacy I may not have had the

## Acknowledgements

opportunity to read and translate *Maria Verum Maria*. Thanks also to Adley Siddiqi and Shefali Jha, faithful first readers, whose comments and suggestions have made this translation better.

And my deepest gratitude to Rahul Soni, editor extraordinaire at HarperCollins India, who championed this book right from the start. His careful and insightful editing proves once again that literary translation is a collaborative endeavour.

Jayasree Kalathil
Hampshire, UK

# About the Author

**Sandhya Mary** is a writer and media professional. Her first book, published in 2011, was a collection of short stories titled *Chittikkaran Yudas Bhoothavarthamana Kalangalkkidayil* (*Chittikkaran Yudas, in Between Past and Present*). *Maria Verum Maria* (2018) is her debut novel. The book, currently in its third edition, established her as a storyteller who engages with serious, topical issues in a light-hearted and humanistic voice.

As a media professional, Sandhya's writings on contemporary social and political issues have been published in various forums including TruecopyThink and *Mathrubhumi* weekend supplement. After receiving her master's degree in communication and journalism, she worked with Indiavision, Kerala's first 24/7 news channel. Currently, she is a producer with Mathrubhumi Club FM.

Sandhya grew up in a predominantly Christian village in Ernakulam district in Kerala, and currently lives in Kochi. She loves to cook, eat and wander around.

# About the Translator

**Jayasree Kalathil** is the author of *The Sackclothman*, a children's book that has been translated into Malayalam, Hindi and Telugu. She shared the JCB Prize for Literature in 2020 with S. Hareesh for her translation of his novel, *Moustache*. She is a recipient of the Crossword Book Award for Indian Language Translation and the V. Abdulla Memorial Translation Prize. Her translation of Sheela Tomy's *Valli* (2022) was shortlisted for the JCB Prize for Literature, the American Literary Translators Association's National Translation Award in Prose, and the Atta Galatta–Bangalore Literature Festival Book of the Year Award.

Originally from Kottakkal in Malappuram district, Kerala, Jayasree currently lives in a small village in the New Forest in England.

# HarperCollins *Publishers* India

At HarperCollins India, we believe in telling the best stories and finding the widest readership for our books in every format possible. We started publishing in 1992; a great deal has changed since then, but what has remained constant is the passion with which our authors write their books, the love with which readers receive them, and the sheer joy and excitement that we as publishers feel in being a part of the publishing process.

Over the years, we've had the pleasure of publishing some of the finest writing from the subcontinent and around the world, including several award-winning titles and some of the biggest bestsellers in India's publishing history. But nothing has meant more to us than the fact that millions of people have read the books we published, and that somewhere, a book of ours might have made a difference.

As we look to the future, we go back to that one word— a word which has been a driving force for us all these years.

Read.